Gazelle Tracks

Gazelle Tracks

MIRAL AL-TAHAWY

A Modern Arabic Novel from Egypt

Translated by Anthony Calderbank

Garnet
PUBLISHING

GAZELLE TRACKS
A Modern Arabic Novel from Egypt

Published by
Garnet Publishing Limited
8 Southern Court
South Street
Reading
RG1 4QS
UK

www.garnetpublishing.co.uk

First Edition

ISBN-13: 978-1-85964-204-7

British Library Cataloguing-in-Publication Data
A catalogue record for this book is available from the British Library

Typeset by Samantha Barden
Jacket design by David Rose
Illustration by Janette Louden

Printed by Biddles, UK

Acknowledgments

———

Many thanks are due to Professor Roger Allen for his thorough revision of an earlier draft of this translation.

———

The publisher would like to thank Moneera Al-Ghadeer, Marilyn Booth, Yasir Suleiman and Muhsin al-Musawi for their generous and invaluable advice and assistance. This series would not have been possible without their support.

Glossary

— —

abaya	cloak-like garment
Amma	title of respect for older women, literally meaning paternal aunt
Ana	title of respect for the mother (Turkish)
arjeela	water pipe
asbah	variety of Arab horse
Bani	sons of, used with tribal names
Baramwa	inhabitants of Barma, a town in the Egyptian Delta
Basha	aristocratic title from the Ottoman Empire, holder of *bashawiyya*
Bin	son of
Bint	daughter of
burgu'	full face veil or mask, sometimes made of leather, worn by the Bedouin women

Esmahan	famous Egyptian singer of the 1930s and 1940s (died 1944)
feddan	a measure of land
Gharabwa	inhabitants of Al-Gharbiyya, a Province of Egypt
gunfus	a desert bird
Hanni	term of respect for a mother or older woman
Hajj	the pilgrimage to Makkah, the title of one who has completed it
igal	black band of cord worn over the *kufiyya*, used metaphorically to refer to Gulf Arabs
jallabiyya	loose-fitting robe worn by Egyptian peasants, with male and female styles
Jidd	grandfather, used as a title for tribal elders and ancestors
Jidda	grandmother
khan	house, inn, trading post
kiswa	the black embroidered covering of the Kaaba in Makkah, traditionally brought from Egypt with the Hajj caravans
kufiyya	man's head cloth worn throughout the Levant and the Gulf, and by Egyptian Bedouins
Layla Murad	legendary Egyptian actress, 1917–1995
liban	traditional chewing gum
majlis	a gathering, a place or room where people sit and meet
makbousa	dish of meat and rice
Manyal Al-Roda	a neighbourhood of Cairo
moulid	festival in honour of a saint

qaftan	ankle-length garment with wide sleeves open at the front
seen	one of the letters of the Arabic alphabet
shunnaf	nose ornament
thobe	an ankle-length garment worn by Bedouin men, with buttons at the neck and cuffs
Ya	said before a person's name when addressing them

1

—·—

Hind was always just a little girl with pigtails and ribbons in her hair. That's how she appeared in the photograph, sitting on a woman's knee. The woman was a Negro lady with jet-black skin and she had a white handkerchief tied round her head and a black veil thrown over the top. She wore a short gown patterned with flowers and around her waist a belt of beads like the gypsy women wear. Underneath the gown were baggy trousers drawn tight at the ankles. I was told that the servant's name was Inshirah. Next to them stood Sagawa, the plump eldest sister, and Sahla, who is still as thin as she was then. Sahla is the one I know best because she has looked after me since I was in nappies, and they were looking for a woman at whose breast I could feed.

Al-Najdiyya isn't in the picture. She must have been somewhere else at the time. Perhaps she was preparing coffee at the large table in the main room where numerous copper cooking pots were set out in a row with one of the servants hunched over them, giving them a good polish. Or maybe she was laying out rugs on the veranda where her guests used to sit, looking out over the huge mulberry trees and the wooden stand for the water urns, and orange saplings where the little bees made such a racket in the spring.

Every where she went Hind carried an exercise book in which she recorded the secrets that no one else knew. Whenever she walked down the garden path, she would sit against the trunk of the Indian mango tree whose fruit they picked first because it ripened before the others. Or she would go and sit among the guava trees at the far end of the plantation. That's where she saw Mutlig fondling Farhana's breasts. The servant girl was tossing about in the dust like a monkey, her chest heaving, as the beads from her necklace flew about in all directions. After that incident another servant girl called Rawda, who was also black, with two short pigtails of matted frizzy hair, related how Mutlig had been waiting for her at the bottom of the hill when she came home in the evening with the animals, holding the halter of the three young fillies in her hand. Hind knew that when they put out the lamp and stopped telling stories, her sisters would slip off to bed and leave the servants in the kitchen. The servants would adjust their straw pillows under their heads and talk about him.

"He's reached puberty," Rawda says. "Boys at that age turn into stallions. They're like male camels on heat."

Inshirah laughs: "What he needs is an hour with Fatima Al-Gurumiyya."

As she hides in the darkness, eavesdropping on the snippets of conversation, Hind tries to imagine how the skinny little boy she sees on feast days and special occasions can do such things. He's still so young. He kisses Al-Najdiyya's hand and calls her "*Ya Hanni*" as the Arabs do instead of "*Ya Ana*" like the Turks, and she pats him on the head and squeezes a copper penny into his palm.

There was only this one picture of Hind in Al-Najdiyya's house, whose walls were covered with faded photographs. No wedding photo of her existed, only this one, of her sitting on the knee of her servant Inshirah, remote and unapproachable, a little girl with pigtails. "Poor thing," they would say as they stood in front of the picture. It was as if they had agreed never to speak about her, and she seemed forever in the distance, far removed from everything that concerned them. Jidda Al-Najdiyya said the words, then added that the last time she had seen Hind, her hair had turned completely white and her body had wasted away. Al-Najdiyya had watched the women pour water over the corpse before wrapping it in the shroud. Then they sprinkled perfume and left. They did not wail or weep or even put on their mourning clothes. They had pronounced her dead long before, from the day they had placed her in that house, shut up the windows and doors and walked away, heedless of her screams. "Poor thing," they said, and then never mentioned her name again. They hurried back to their homes, but from that day forth, Hind would come to them. The first time they saw her she was running round the yard. Muhra was resting in Al-Najdiyya's lap as the old woman told her the story of Al-Suha, the mother gazelle that ran across the night sky. She had abandoned one of her little ones on the open sand and because it did not know how to escape from the hunter, she had left her shining tracks as bright stars to lead it to safety. Al-Najdiyya spreads out her fingers to show the times of misfortune when the new moon appears with Al-Suha to its right, and the days of the dust storms when the moon is full, and Sirius is in the south and Al-Suha in the middle. That is how Al-Najdiyya chronicles times of hardship and times of prosperity.

Muhra looked at Hind as she ran in front of them, a little girl with pigtails in the form of a cat. Al-Najdiyya turned to Sahla who was sitting beside her:

"Sahla my girl," she said, "the baby comes from the belly not the heart."

Sahla, who was leaning against the column on the terrace, took Muhra, rested the little girl's head in her own lap, and began to run her fingers through her hair, plaiting it as she recited spells and charms. Hind started to come more often. She would lick Muhra's feet and wake her up, and Muhra would hold her in her arms and go back to sleep to her purring. She scratched the rug and tore out thick strands with her claws but when Muhra told them about it they patted her on the shoulder and told her it was all in her imagination. Muhra started to cry all the time. She was convinced that she was walking naked through a vast white void while Hind flew around her like a moth. Muhra pretended not to take the apparitions seriously but deep inside she was sure that when the dogs barked, they had seen Hind just as she had, whether it was as a moth or a bird or a cat licking her feet, and she knew that Hind came to the others too. It was Hind that kissed Sagawa on her mouth to bid her farewell before she passed away, and Hind whom Al-Najdiyya saw tucking her up in bed before they closed her eyes and said: "God rest her soul."

2

— ‐ —

Muhra doesn't know who named her mother Sahla. At the Mère de Dieu, where Al-Najdiyya took the three sisters and handed them over to Mademoiselle Anita, they called her Rose. For eight years she kept that name until Lamloum Basha Al-Basil came to kiss his little girls at the last school party, collect their bags and take them back to where Al-Najdiyya sat on her rug on the veranda. On the Bedouin estates by the bank of the canal, the girls still had land and stables and a traditional goat-hair tent in a courtyard surrounded on every side by mango groves and orange trees. Of the three girls it was Hind who liked to wear tight trousers and straw hats with roses round the brim. Later, when I saw the other photographs, there was a large one of her playing in the stable with a black girl, one of the slaves they called the slaves of Clan Minazi'. That was how they were known before they discovered that there were other, far richer masters and Mubarak the Slave packed them off to work in that land far away where oil comes out of the ground and where they

5

could excel, as they always had, at skinning sheep and boiling coffee with cardamom and spices, and massaging legs with warm water and fresh basil. They were highly skilled at lighting fires and knew many things about hawks and falcons: like how to clean the bird's leg so it doesn't develop sores, and how to reward fillies with pieces of sugar, and how to tame salukis. They remained proficient in all of these matters as long as those who employed them were worthy of their loyalty and attention, and didn't just drool over nostalgic tales of ancient glories that were gone forever.

Princess Muhra, daughter of the Clan Al-Shafei (that was their nickname for her) moved to Al-Najdiyya's house, where Hind, Sagawa and Sahla used to live. Her father, Mutlig, would spend the day reclining outside the goat-hair tent, resting his head on Amma Mizna's leg.

"*Ya* Mazzoun," he would say, "may Allah have mercy on your parents. Your great grandfather Al-Shafei travelled with the caravans from Sinnar to Qous and from Qift to Aydhab and there was not a single person who dared to throw sand in his camels' faces."

Amma Mizna, who was the only one of his many sisters still alive, would turn up on her donkey with two saddlebags in which she packed jerked meat, buttermilk and hard salted cheese for his long journeys. She was the one who taught Muhra how to sit like a Bedouin woman on the rug and who wove little dolls for her out of sheep's wool and sewed wings on them. She used to sit Muhra on her knee as she chuckled and pretended to be a camel running along, and she would sing her a song:

> You're not an easy prey to catch,
> No tender lamb for the shepherd to snatch

in order to remind her that she was a daughter of the Arabs, a true desert thoroughbred. Her grandfather, Al-Shafei Al-Sulaymi, was a noble and generous man, more generous than the legendary Hatim Al-Ta'i, whose story they related in their tales. He was a proud man too. Once, when one of his wives decided to leave him, he galloped over to the hill they called Al-Aliya where she had fled and fired his shotgun at her. He was completely mad. There were a number of palm trees in the wide courtyard in front of his house and he used to sit in their shade. Whenever anyone riding an animal passed by his gate, he would have them dismount and look at the ground as they walked by. It was said that he had tied many of the Gharabwa to these palm trees and flogged them because they were uncouth savages and did not know the rules. In the days before electricity came to our land, he used to light his fire then ride round the people's homes asking them: "Whose fire is that, my boy?" Anyone who did not know the fire of Clan Al-Shafei would be tied to the palm trees and flogged. Then he would come back to sit at the head of his *majlis* and curse the times when men no longer had character or breeding. Many of the young men considered him crazy, for he still believed that it was his fire the exhausted caravans sought out so that he could shower them with hospitality, and all the time motorcars sped past him on the asphalt highway.

It was this grandfather who left his goat-hair tent to my father along with a number of salukis, his falconry tackle and some *feddans* of land which he divided up among his many sons. He was especially keen that one of his sons should head his *majlis* after his death, and my father was the one who took upon himself that task, even though he had been educated at Victoria College and had almost taken a degree in English Literature. Father loved sitting round the fire with the taste of smoke in his throat. That's where he spent most of his time, with Surour and Mubarak the Slave by his side, along with many others who enjoyed smoking certain potent substances and drinking coffee with opium dissolved in it. They would mull over stories about members of the family, especially the great grandfather and his hunting trips in the marshes around the Bitter Lakes, or the grandfather on mother's side, Minazi', and his journeys to the land of black mud and the Sudan. Father was a great raconteur. He had committed some of Goethe's poems to memory and it was he who taught me Shakespeare's plays in excellent English with a vibrant theatrical voice that thrilled me to the core.

Nevertheless, despite all his culture, her father did not agree with boarding schools and he told Muhra that they had ruined the mind of her mother and aunts. It was he who came up with the ridiculous suggestion that Muhra should go to the Minazi' Estate Primary School carried on the shoulder of a black slave girl, the daughter of one of the sons of Mubarak the Slave. Her name was Nawwar and she used to sit Muhra in the front row, having given clear instructions that no one should sit next to her. Most of the teachers, who were aware that she bore her grandfather's name, respected the wish of her mother, the daughter of Lamloum Basha Al-Basil, that Muhra should not learn anything offensive, especially since all the children around her were mere peasants. Amma Mizna, who knew everyone in the village and how each was related to the other, would actually say of them: "Our dear friends who have always been our servants." She said the word "servants" with humility, as if it were an honour they should feel fortunate to enjoy. Some of the new teachers looked in curiosity, even disbelief, at Nawwar, who sat by the classroom door waiting for her charge. One of them even had the audacity to lift Muhra down from the classroom window, where she had sat one day swinging her legs over the edge of the sill and singing at the top of her voice:

> With all his many camels
> He lives a noble life.
> And fine and handsome sons he has
> And not a moment's strife

The teacher grabbed her by the arms: "Do you think you're on your father's estate?" he demanded to know. Her father came and told the hapless teacher that it was indeed his estate and her grandfather's before him. The land had been theirs since the sun first blazed down on the shifting sand, and not even a genie would dare to pass across it. They had been his masters when his forefathers were eating shit in their wretched little villages which were ravaged by famine and typhus and the river wasn't even wide enough to dump the bodies of people like him in it. Meanwhile his grandfather, Minazi', whom the school was named after, had ridden his stallion from east to west and opened up this wasteland. The teacher, who appeared slightly unable to grasp all this, was advised by his colleagues to apologise, because they were "Arabs" and stubborn characters; they might do anything if they felt their pride had been offended. Father was not totally convinced with their assurances and one evening the unfortunate primary school burnt down while he was relaxing in his pavilion sipping copious amounts of steaming coffee and poking the embers. The fire solved the problem of the seat on the front row and a carpet was spread out in the sandy courtyard for all to sit on, without seats or chairs. It was also a great relief for Nawwar, for she had grown fed up of carrying Muhra to school every day once her young mistress had learned to run there and back by herself. In any case the school was right next to the wall of their house and opposite the houses of other folk whom Muhra was told were her uncles.

Father was generous in his own way, and had decided that he would sit in front of his pavilion, light a fire and skin a sheep. Sitting around him were Surour and Mubarak and some enthusiastic young men who were always talking about grand social projects that would preserve the good name of the family. Mutlig was also very generous when it came to selling small portions of his *feddans* at rates very favourable to the buyer, most of whom were Gharabwa or Baramwa (as the people from Barma on the borders of Al-Gharbiyya were known). Apparently the majority of the locals there were famous for raising poultry and selling eggs. Most of those who came were short, fair-skinned women carrying crates on their heads. They would sit themselves down in front of the pavilion and say: "*Ya* Sheikh Al-Arab" in a funny accent. Then they would immediately unfold the handkerchief in which they kept their dirty, rolled-up bank notes and count them out with great deliberation before agreeing on minuscule instalments to be paid back over a long period of time, none of which would enable him to embark upon his project as he had planned. His original intention had been to fill the empty stables that stood next to the house with "pure thoroughbreds," but the structures were no more than derelict feeding troughs and half of them had fallen down. In their place he hoped to build a stud farm befitting the family's illustrious history, sell a few more scraps of land and then buy more original thoroughbreds. Sitting next to him on the rug Amma Mizna would egg him on, her *shunnaf* nose ornament shaking as she nodded her head in agreement at the names he chose for the horses.

"*Ya* Mazzoun," he'd say to her, "your grandfather Al Shafei's mare was called Zad Al-Rakb, like Hatem Al Ta'i's.

She was blond, as yellow as the wheat in the fields. Your grandfather Minazi' used to say that if you gathered all the horses of the Arabs for a race and set them off all at once, the blond would win. The blond is most patient, my father's daughter."

"Your grandfather Minazi"s filly was called Zaafarana," Amma Mizna would respond. "When she was young she used to prance in front of the goat-hair tents. People say that Zaafarana was as black as the night with a white flash on her muzzle and white bands round her fetlocks, but her offspring were few."

They would spend ages debating the merits of the blond and the black. Father would spend even longer driving merrily round the territory of the Huwaytat, Hawara and Juhaina tribes in his Land Rover in search of fillies fit to bear pure progeny. He would stand in front of each horse and inspect its muzzle, which should be broad, and assess the length of its neck and legs and the look of the withers. He always maintained that the Arab horse has a small head and dark eyes, and insisted on checking the genealogies, confirming them by the length of the neck. An authentic mare drinks without bending its forelegs, whereas one of mixed descent kneels slightly to reach the water. After a number of trips he failed to discover such pure thoroughbreds and he realised that many of the bloodlines had been mixed with outside strains. He gave in and convinced himself that a filly's family tree wasn't absolutely necessary. Instead he decided to exercise his intuition, and guess the purity of his purchases simply by eyeing them up and down.

Once again he consulted Amma Mizna about the bay and the black and why his fillies were ill starred. Immediately Amma sat down on the floor and announced that the *asbah*, which is the colour of the early morning, is too common, while the bay, whose colour inclines towards red, does not produce many offspring. From now on he should keep away from short backs and check carefully the length of the belly and make sure the limbs are well-proportioned, for now he has acquired a number of fillies and a stable lad to lead them. With his evening water pipe bubbling in the background he had long conversations about their names: Igab, Al-Sumay, Janah, Al-Balqa'. And he thumbed at length through the records of his forefathers looking for those famous sayings which he hoped might bring Sahla Bint Minazi' round to his way of thinking as she sat on the veranda: sayings such as: "We prefer chargers to children," and "See to your horses, for they are the fastness of the Arabs."

Sahla, however, was more concerned with the women who continued to count out their bank notes and inquire after this plot of land or that, and she did not comment. She left him with Amma Mizna in the goat-hair tent, to share boiling coffee during the day and the crackling fire in the pavilion in the evening. Muhra was happy to inspect her father's fillies, while Sahla withdrew into silent disdain, which could be seen quite clearly, for example, in the way she contemplated his trembling fingers as he poured her coffee in the morning. Perhaps it was in consolation that he would recite a verse of poetry; he said it so often that Muhra memorised it without understanding its meaning:

> A man can fall on hard times if he's too kind
> And foolish and weak will he be defined,
> But money comes back to where it has been,
> Like a branch once bare is clothed again in green.

Sahla shook her head, convinced that it was a waste of time to even try and change him. After he had bought the horses the house began to receive delegations of Arabs from the Gulf; Saudis and Kuwaitis that Surour and Mubarak the Slave brought. These guests required that more sheep be slaughtered, and the reception hall had to be painted so they might have the opportunity to peruse the photographs: Jidd Minazi' on a hunting trip with his shotgun slung over his shoulder, King Saud with the Arab sheikhs of Egypt and a red circle round Jidd Al-Shafei as he raises his forehead proudly in the middle of the picture, this grandfather or that one congratulating his Highness on the birth of the heir to the throne, or the anniversary of his accession, and the deed of ownership to land in the Sinai Peninsula belonging to Great Grandfather Mahjoub. My father loved talking about his fillies too. He would swear that Al-Sahba' was pure Arab, and he spent ages researching her genealogy: "When it comes to the lines of an original thoroughbred it's a matter of necessity." At this juncture he might also tell his guests how he ended up marrying Muhra's mother, Sahla Bint Lamloum Basha Minazi', who, as his cousin, was rightfully his even though he didn't ask for her. Muhra wondered why he never mentioned Hind, who was also his cousin, but all he would say was:

"Even if she's in the howdah on her way to wed a stranger, she'll jump down and marry her cousin if only he says the word." The visitors would nod their heads as he underlined the point: "We'd sooner throw her to the crocodiles than have her marry a peasant."

He tells them the story of Jidd Mahjoub who threw his daughter into the river after Abbas I, King of Egypt, asked for her hand in marriage. He can't remember her name exactly, but assures them that she was even fairer than Al-Jaziya, noble heroine of the Bani Hilal epic. Her neck was as slender as a she-camel's, and she was a true daughter of the Arabs. She could never accept a red-faced Turk like him even if he were the son of the Sultan himself. He was obliged to repeat more stories, to light fire after fire, serve coffee after coffee, slaughter even more sheep, and summon Surour, Mubarak and Nawwar from their homes to say that they were the slaves of Clan Minazi'. Then he brought the brass coffee-pots stained with green blotches out of the cupboard to polish them, and insisted on pitching a goat-hair tent in the middle of the courtyard. These sessions regularly ended with the summoning of one of the women from Barma so she could give my father a few guineas, the proceeds of his latest agreement to sell another plot of land somewhere or other.

As for Muhra, the business of her sitting on the sand in the schoolyard was only resolved when the school was rebuilt after the adjacent land was bought from one of her paternal uncles. After all the legal procedures had been completed, they removed the old sign and put in its place one which read: "Rif'at Abdul Hayy Modern Primary School." Her father submitted numerous petitions to the Education Authority denouncing such blatant contempt for their heritage and genealogy and the utter distortion of historical facts. He demanded to know where this Abdul Hayy character had been when all this land was just acres of dry sand inherited over the years by the sons of Great Grandfather Mahjoub. When they told him that Rif'at Abdul Hayy had been a commander in the fifth battalion of guards, and was a hero of the revolution, father went home and slumped against the pavilion wall. He didn't say a word, just sat there drawing lines in the sand with a dry stick in his trembling hand.

It was her mother who finally insisted she left the school. Sahla packed her bags, having decided to leave the village for the house she had inherited in Manyal Al-Roda overlooking the Nile. It was an old house built in the thirties, with high windows. She left father to supervise his fillies as they cantered round the courtyard and Amma Mizna tested out her cupping remedies, set broken legs and calmed the stubborn fillies by rubbing rose oil on their muzzles. Mutlig and Mizna could have all the conversations they wanted about offspring and breeding and weaning the yearlings from the mares.

3

— • —

Muhra's grandfather on her father's side, whose picture they'd hung on one end of the wall, was called Al-Shafei. She would tell people that Al-Shafei's folk hailed from the territory of Bani Sulaym, and that when her father went on the pilgrimage he met people who told him about that region, and that the tribes there owned a breed of horse known as Al-A'waj. It is a small horse with extremely long legs, so long in fact that it bends them while it is asleep. When my father came back with a pile of prayer beads and distributed them at his *majlis* in the pavilion, they addressed him: "*Ya* Hajj." He adjusted his *abaya* and declared:

"Among all the Arabs there is no horse more renowned of name nor greater of lineage, no more copious a producer of offspring nor more commonly mentioned in their poetry, than it."

"Than who, *Ya* Sheikh Al-Arab?" they all asked.

"Al-A'waj, the desert charger of Bani Sulaym," he replied grinning with pride. "The lineage goes back to the stallion of Nu'man Bin Al-Mundhir, whose name was Al-Yahmoum. Its mother was the filly which the Prophet of Allah rode at the battle of Badr, whose name was Al-Sama."

They shake their heads in awe as their eyes wander over to our empty stables. Then there is talk of reviving the Bedouin heritage by building a racetrack where the fillies could run against one another with the salukis bounding behind them.

Once, on father's first attempt to drive to the resort of Marsa Matrouh, we got lost. He pulled up where some Bedouins had camped and got out of the car. A middle-aged man was sitting in front of one of the tents pounding coffee beans. My father sat down in front of him, lent forward and said that he was a Sulaymi, from Bani Sulaym, the brothers of Hilal. The Sheikh told him that there had been Bani Sulaym living there at Maryout, and in the surrounding country, after they returned from Al-Jabal Al-Akhdar in Libya, but Bani Hilal had run them out and chased them over the river to the eastern side. Then Muhammad Ali had removed them to the south. My father turned over his coffee cup and began to correct this version of the migrations from the west to the east then to the south. In the end he took his pistol out of its holster and announced that Bani Hilal were "animal dung," roaming from country to country and were it not for the sword of Bani Sulaym they would never have dared cross to the west of the Nile, nor would they have been able to stand up to Al-Zinati Khalifa. The battle between Sulaym and Hilal raged for another two hours on the lips of my father and that Sheikh, who in the end drove us away as if he were shooing his sheep. We drove round for more than three hours with no idea how to get out of the scrub land that was dotted with treacherous marshes, wild plants and clumps of trees, and nothing but barren desert beyond. We finally managed to reach the coast with the help of some shepherds we stumbled upon.

On another occasion my father decided to cross Al-Jabal Al-Akhdar in his Volkswagen and met lots of people who told him about Sulaym and Hilal and their long struggle over a well named Hedaywa. He spent the whole trip investigating the events of those days and gathered many verses of poetry which he entitled: "A Collection of Folk Verses Containing the Compositions of the Poet of Bani Sulaym Regarding an Incident of Ignominious Deceit."

My other grandfather, whose picture my mother hung next to Al-Shafei's picture, but in a more expensive frame, was his brother. Nevertheless I often saw fierce battles erupt over the two frames. My mother was immensely proud that her father had been awarded the title of Basha, while my father's father had remained a camel herdsman with cracked heels living in a tent, lighting his fire, running with his salukis, and asking passers by: "Whose fire is that, my boy?" When he died he did not leave a pair of racing binoculars or an Italian watch with a gold chain by Gautinio.

My mother's father would sit on the veranda of the house he had built in the village. It was made of brick and had a roof of wooden beams, and he had surrounded it with trees, flower beds and pigeon towers, and he had lined the drive with buansiyana and jazourina. His name was Lamloum, and I don't know why but they always added the adjective Al-Basil (which means "fearless"), to his name – before he was granted the title Basha, that is – and followed that with Al-Minazi', the clan name.

Lamloum Basha Al-Minazi' always sat on the veranda smoking his *arjeela*. Sitting at his feet on the rug was a veteran Sheikh called Abu Shreek Al-Iyadi who had been a guide for Old Minazi''s caravans, and by his side another man named Mubarak the Slave. They said he was one of the slaves of Clan Minazi'. In the reception hall was that photograph I kept looking at: three girls with coloured ribbons in their hair, all wearing the same school uniform. In another photograph there was a boy standing alone playing with a young filly's mane. Al-Najdiyya would be sat in the hall on a large rug amid the cushions, legs crossed, calling to the young servant girl to fetch her medicine chest, which contained a large mirror, an eyebrow pencil, and a sky blue bottle of perfume. When the perfume was finished I used to collect the empty bottles. It was called Le Soir. Al-Najdiyya was always chewing bitter gum and mastic and a few cloves. Under her headscarf her soft hair was the colour of henna, and it covered the edge of one eyebrow, pulled back with a grip just below the eyelid.

The Basha used to follow the news broadcasts on the radio with great interest. They had been talking about revolutionary correctionism and agricultural reform. Then one day thirty men came through the gate. Abu Shreek said they were Gharabwa. They attacked the vineyards and the Baghdadi dates, and the cypresses, poplars and chestnut trees, which he had brought back from his travels. They chased the brightly coloured peacocks and the gazelles round their pens. One of them jumped onto the back of the giraffe that the Basha had acquired on one of his journeys to Darfour. The pens, which were covered with chicken wire and had dogs guarding them, were all plundered before Mubarak the slave realised what was going on and fired a few shots into the air with his shotgun. Abu Shreek chased the men off with his stick, running after them as they trampled through the rare flower garden and the clumps of jasmine, before he finally sat down by the wall.

"What has become of the decent people in the world?" he wailed. And he swore on the head of Jidd Minazi', who had terrified the wild beasts in the jungle, that he would teach those Gharabwa peasants a lesson; they were no better than worms crawling about in the earth. The Basha had arranged everything in readiness to receive His Majesty, should he wish to go out and hunt, or to provide a suitable lifestyle for one of his daughters should she become a princess, such as Sahla, my mother. He went inside the house, locked the doors and sat in front of the picture of Jidd Minazi'. He gazed at the map of the estates along the banks of the river that had been given to the tribe by His Majesty. In return they secured the passage of the caravans from Birkat Al Hajj on the outskirts of Cairo as far as Gaza in the north and Al-Qaseer and Al-Qalzam in the south, protecting them from tribes that plundered everything that passed in the vicinity of Wadi Al Qubab and Mount Sinai. The royal decree confirming the tribe's guardianship of the Nile caravans still hung on the wall of that richly furnished lounge where he had met Saad Zaghloul Basha, the King, Baron Empain, Prince Abdul Muhsin, and Prince Faisal Al Saud: on that particular occasion they had discussed the strong genealogical ties between the Shammar and Anza tribes, and Bani Sulaym.

There were lots of photographs covering the walls. The one of Hind sitting on her nanny's lap with Sahla and Sagawa on either side had always hung next to a picture, or rather a large painting, by an artist they say was Dutch, and sometimes French. His name was Pierre Kamm. He had painted a traditional Bedouin evening gathering. The dancer, her face covered by a *burgu'*, sways seductively in front of a row of men who are clapping the rhythm for her. In the background behind them a caravan of camels carrying howdahs disappears into the distance. Next to that was the picture of the boy stroking his filly. His name is Nafidh, brother of the three sisters. He became the distant uncle after Jidd Lamloum sent him to study law in Paris. A few months after he left he sent them a picture of his wedding in

California or New Jersey (they didn't know the difference), with all the cards and telegrams of congratulation, and a photograph of his Lebanese wife. They had opened a petrol station together after he had sought power of attorney to sell all the land he had inherited. Every few years he would send his mother some photos. The last one was of his daughter whom he called Sofi. He told my mother that he sometimes called the girl Hind because his dead sister came to him a lot and he could never forget that he was the one who had caused it all to happen. When I asked my mother about that last sentence she wouldn't say a word. She simply folded up the letters and sighed, but Hind still came to play with my hair and miaow.

The house with the high windows looked out over the boats sailing past. Through the opaque glass you could see the Nile on one side and a narrow bustling street filled with shops and stalls on the other. This is where Muhra would grow up and fall in love. Her mother would sit beside her on the balcony watching the feluccas drift by while a young girl sitting on the floor at her feet polished the pictures Sahla had taken down off the old walls. She would let her restless mind settle on the mysterious canvas and the steady clapping which emanated from the frame in celebration of the charms of the veiled woman who glided up and down in front of the men like a phantom. When my mother re-emerged from her trance in front of the picture she would talk about the annual sale of the citrus fruits, and the price of mangoes and oranges.

She had been left the house, Al-Najdiyya's house, by Lamloum Basha, together with a large garden and a number of court cases involving the Department of Agricultural Reform, for after the raid the land had been divided up among the peasants and turned into a large colony of over two hundred families. It was impossible to evict anyone who had bought, sold or inherited. Nevertheless my mother continued to follow the cases while my father sold his last plots. Then he wrote a lengthy memorandum to His Majesty King Faisal Bin Abdulaziz Al Saud. In it he explained how, in the days when the Arabian Peninsula waited for the caravan bearing the *kiswa* from Egypt, Bani Sulaym had stood beside their brethren from Shammar and Anza before the good times came and had opened their pastures to their brothers for more than a century. It was now time for Bani Sulaym to return to their territories in the Najd, and to take their share of the bounty that had flowed in abundance for all. He noted that he had in his possession more than one document confirming his Hijazi roots as well as a number of deeds recognising the allegiance through good times and bad, some signed by Bin Saud others by Nouri Bin Sha'lan, Grand Sheikh of the Rowla Tribes who inhabited Northern Hijaz as far as the Jordan River. And to prove his Arab roots, he attached some faded photographs of his two grandfathers, Jidd Al-Shafei and Jidd Minazi' hunting gazelles at Al-Alagi and Al-Qalzam, together with others of tethered Arab horses, slaves carrying falcons on their forearms and embers for coffee at their feet. He also enclosed a petition with the signatures of over two thousand members of the clan. But despite all that he received no reply.

He continued to frequent the embassy and the foreign ministry, presenting a similar petition in which he sought permission to emigrate or return to the ancestral lands. Then he discovered after a few months that what he was asking for was impossible and that no one was paying him the slightest bit of attention. Amma Mizna warmed him up a piece of barley bread over the embers and reminded him of his standing and renown while he cracked the knuckles of his trembling hands: Jidd Al-Shafei had galloped his horse from Al-Alawaya to the land of black mud and the Sudan, and no one dared stand in his way. My father fingered his prayer beads and muttered:

Never did such dire tribulation upon a man alight,
Darker now is my despair than the darkest pitch-black night.

He continued to watch his plot of land that the Baramwa and
the Gharabwa and the sons of Mizayna and others had
enclosed with mud walls, behind which they had built low
houses and cut paths and roads between their doors. He
wandered up and down the narrow lanes looking for a
camphor tree he had once planted on a wooded part of his
land, or the mulberry that stood on Al-Shafei canal. He came
across some men cutting away part of its trunk to make
way for the extension of the main road which connected the
buildings to the highway. Then they removed the sign saying
"Rab' Minazi'" and replaced it with one saying "Izbit Al-Tel."
Meanwhile Amma Mizna continued to clip the hair of a
single she-camel and work on the cloak she'd been trying to
finish for the previous ten years. As she did so she recited the
ballad of Al-Shafei or Minazi' or Mahjoub Al-Kabir who had
been thrown into the river in a sack. She changed the name at
the start of the story as she pleased. And so they went on, sitting
in the goat-hair tent, talking about the fillies he'd tethered in
the yard and how they weren't fertile yet; the only one that
had delivered was that young filly he hadn't even chosen a
name for. In spite of all Amma Mizna's efforts in following up
this matter of offspring as they sat on the sheepskin rug in the
yard, they concluded in the end that horses are like women,
or new houses, some bring bad luck, some bring good.

None of the horses my father bought brought him the
good fortune he had been waiting for. The guests from the
Gulf who came with Surour the Slave to look at the stables
shifted their *igals* to the left and right and spoke about German
stables, Belgian stud-farms, the British royal family's horses
and auctions in Oxford and London. They did not think my

father's horses were even worth the trouble of looking at. They simply expressed their surprise that there were still Arab tribes in this part of the world that maintained the genealogies and lines of their horses. My father who, with his photos and documents, and his coffee pots and petitions, was ready to return to the Hijaz, found no one to heed his call save a gentlemen they called Prince Lubad. He dragged my father off his sheepskin rug next to the empty stables to join him on his hunting trips and hawking expeditions. The Prince thought father would bring him good luck, as an expert with the birds of prey. Together they travelled on a long journey, from the Alps to catch white falcons, to the Singar Mountains in Uzbekistan and Turkmenistan, and then to remote parts of Canada and Australia. My father loved flying and possessed great skill at sipping coffee and poking the fire. He had small, keen eyes and was able to estimate the age and breeding of a bird from the first look. Indeed, he appeared to be an expert on all birds of prey, their seasons and habitats, and more experienced still in setting broken feathers. His sharp eyes would survey the hunting ground to ascertain the presence of snakes. He had explored lots of places, and sold all his land, only to end up driving an old jeep from Wadi Natroun and Al-Alamein to Wadi Al-Rayyan and Lake Qaroun with Surour and Mubarak by his side. During his lifetime he had spent endless days chasing vultures and second rate hawks that did not know how to hunt, in the hope of catching a pair of sakers he could sell for a few thousand guineas and restore his former glory. But all he managed to trap were bustards and jerboas.

Hunting with Prince Lubad was a new experience. Mutlig and his men had used a simple horsehair net tied to the back of a pigeon in the hope that a hawk circling in the sky might swoop down: as its claws clutched at the pigeon they became entangled in the net. The men ran over to the spot where the birds fell and covered the hawk with their cloaks. Hunting with the Prince on the other hand was a magnificent battle, chasing the birds with wirelesses and automatic rifles while checking their position with global positioning devices. That's why my father was content to deal with the situation not as a falconer but rather as an expert on birds of prey.

"The white bird is a delight to the eye," he would say as he fingered his prayer beads, "and the black is ill-tempered. The red is a great hunter. Green falcons are the worst type but the spotted Nidawi is good for hunting gazelles."

He might also have told them about Jidd Minazi' and how he caught monkeys and ostriches in the Sudan, or that Jidd Al-Shafei had a Singari hawk which he called Al Qannou', that lived with him for ten years. And as his audience turned over their coffee cups he would contemplate the hall which Prince Lubad had filled with all kinds of different coloured birds, but left to his slaves the tasks of filling their feeding troughs with pigeons, cleaning their talons and training them to hunt gazelle.

When my father returned from his long sojourn with the Prince he hung a sign over the door which said "Mutlig Al-Shafei Al-Sulaymi, Equestrian and Falconry Expert." He had some cards printed for Mubarak to give to his guests who came to hunt gazelles in Wadi Al-Alaqi. He hammered a wooden block into the ground and tethered a baby vulture to it, and put a few wild bustards and some pigeons in a cage. And he started to talk of better ways to keep up the good name of the clan and projects that would restore its glory, like holding a regular assembly, or starting a newspaper in the tribe's name whose slogan would be: "Bedouinism: the origin of civilization."

4

—-

There is no photograph of the grandfather to both my
mother and father. His name was Younis. He was the
brother of Al-Shafei and Minazi'. He was born in the Syrian
Desert after the tribes were driven north. My father said they
had sought help from Al-Shareef Abdullah; my mother said
it was from Nouri Al-Sha'lan, head of the Rowla Tribes. The
incident erupted over a young woman named Khayaliyya;
Amma Mizna used to sing a ballad about her as she bounced
me up and down on her knees:

> You're not the prey of hunters,
> Nor born to be a slave.
> Your ancestors all were free men,
> Great heroes, gallant and brave.

They had thrown her into the river for the crocodiles to eat so
that she would forever remain a thoroughbred and not be

mounted by a peasant, even if he were Abbas I, son of the Sultan of Egypt.

"Abbas's regiments were in hot pursuit on racing camels," one of my uncles used to relate. "They chased us as we fled through the desert with our women until we reached the Khan." My father's paternal aunt, whose name I don't know, said that the sheikh who led us through the desert was called Younis, and that Abbas had sent an agent after him who stabbed him in the back at the Khan. But there are other accounts which say that Sattam, who was the nephew of one of Younis's brothers, was actually the one who stabbed him in the back. So they called the spot Khan Younis, which means the place where Younis was betrayed, and said that Sattam committed the deed in order to become sheikh of the Arab tribes.

It was Younis who swore an oath of blood brotherhood with Mansour Al-Mizayni, Sheikh of the Mizayna tribes, in the Syrian Desert. For decades the two of them exchanged olives, oil and bars of soap from Aleppo for silk, fine cloth and barley from the land of the Copts. They say that it was Lamloum Al-Basil who settled the Mizayna tribes in his territory after they fled from the Jews who were moving into Palestine.

"*Ya* Sheikh Al-Arab," they said, "We are joined in allegiance by ties of blood."

Lamloum Basha pitched a tent for them near his guest quarters and when it became too small for them they built mud houses and yards in Rab' Minazi'. Their camels continued to come and go with the Hajj caravans and merchants' expeditions, and at harvest times.

When Amma Fatima Al-Mizayniyya used to come to my father's *majlis*, Amma Mizna would call her "the guest." "The guest said," she would report, "the guest went, the guest sat down." Yet they were no longer guests. They had become our neighbours, and whenever we had an evening of Arab singing and hand clapping, Amma Fatima would come along and sing some traditional Bedouin ballads:

A ravishing maiden, noble born
She turns the heads of young and old,
Like rich cloths in the Jewish quarter,
Dyed colours bright and bold.

And when there was a bereavement and the women stained their faces black, Amma Fatima would come round with her sister Maryam to beat the funeral drum and wail laments with my grandmothers:

His threshold it was famous,
Folk came from far and wide.
But now the door is closed
No more we'll step inside.

Amma Fatima would come round to pound blocks of kohl, alum and mastic, and talk about the homelands of Anza, the territories of Mizayna and the camping grounds of Huwaytat. She always rounded off her stories by saying: "Allah have mercy on our folk and your folk. They were noble and generous, valiant to a man."

Amma Fatima was Al-Najdiyya's only friend. When Al-Najdiyya came from Kafr Al-Zayyat in a howdah with a caravan of camels like a true Arab daughter they fired shots into the air for seven days. The women soon discovered that this daughter of the noble Najdi clan of Al-Jibali was a civilised woman who could do her eyebrows with a black pencil and took snuff up her long straight nose. Lamloum Basha was proud of his wife, for even though she was a pure-bred filly, she didn't wear the black *burgu'* and her eyes were always lined seductively with kohl, and a lock of soft hair stuck out from underneath her headscarf. A golden pendant hung in the centre of her forehead and she looked like a Turkish princess. She knew how to make pigeon casserole, and ratatouille and she stuffed sheep with wild thyme and pistachios, put camphor leaves in the earthen tray under the water urns and dissolved essence of rose in the water, and she placed henna leaves between her folded clothes.

All of this was a stunning revelation among the wide mud houses where the highest expression of the culinary art was to crumble some corn flour into curdled milk and pour black honey on top. A sheep and a few crumbs of bread was all the villagers and their guests could expect. Al-Najdiyya found that she shared common interests with Jidda Fatima. Together they bottled mango juice after sweetening and sealed it with wax, and made marmalade that was the talk of the entire hamlet. Amma Fatima Al-Mizayniyya massaged Al-Najdiyya's back for her with crushed camphor leaves and olive oil and managed to cure almost all her aches and pains.

That's how her name became associated with that of Sagawa, who is the one standing to the right of Inshirah in the photograph, plump, a little taller than Sahla, not as beautiful as Hind but more so than Sahla. They never said "poor thing" about Sagawa, even though she was the first to pass away, and had spent most of her life succumbing to fits. She would fall to the ground, cold-limbed, with her features contracted. They had hung a sapphire on her forehead to make the pain go away and dressed her in green silk so her mind would be calm and the evil spirits would depart, but to no avail. Al-Najdiyya looked in all the villages for an amethyst to soothe Sagawa's heart, and they tattooed a green fish on her temple and made incisions above her eyebrows, but still she could be sitting there like a docile cat one minute and be lying on the floor stiff as a board the next. The fits never left her alone and time after time she fell down. And even though they had forbidden her from going into the kitchens and moving about on her own, once she fell on the iron bed post, once on the fire, and another time on a tray of coffee cups. Then she fell for the last time against one of the stone balusters that looked like clay jars. They all gathered round her as the blood flowed across the veranda floor and moths flew into the lamps on the ceiling, their wings sizzling with a smell like lamb roasting.

Amma Fatima knew the details of that story that they had all tried to hide. Perhaps she had been with Al-Najdiyya and heard the Basha saying: "He's no better than a dog," as Sagawa lay there, stretched out on the floor with her white legs all exposed. Sahm's eyes were transfixed on the *thobe* that had ridden up to reveal Sagawa's body. Inshirah nursed Sahm from one breast while she fed Uncle Nafidh from the other. Al-Najdiyya always maintained that slaves' milk makes a man strong in contrast to a girl who should never be fed by a slave. Sahm ran around like a puppy with the little girls in the photograph. They jumped off the bales of cotton that were being loaded into huge sacks and stacked in rows in Al-Najdiyya's yard as the prices were negotiated. Sahm's skinny legs knocked together like monkeys in the land of black mud. When they played hide and seek he always found Sagawa's hiding place; she would roll around, hidden among the sacks, and he would grab her pigtails. That was before he grew up. Then he addressed the young girls as "My master's daughter" and lowered his eyes as he passed them.

Nevertheless Sahm was still allowed to go between the two yards, the yard of the house and the yard of the pavilion

where the men had their *majlis*. In and out of the kitchen he
went, carrying coffee-pots and trays of food arranged along his
arm, then he would hold Nafidh's filly while the young master
mounted up. Sahm isn't in any of the photographs, however,
and when I asked what he looked like they would simply say:
"A slave, one of the slaves of Clan Minazi'." Perhaps he looked
like Inshirah, or Nawwar, his sister, or had other features they
didn't want to mention. They say he had another name but
that the Basha called him Sahm (which means arrow) because
when they were out hunting he could move faster than the
salukis. He would run after a bird that had been hit by shot
and catch it before it hit the ground. Fatima Al-Mizayniyya
said that Sahm was crouching on top of Sagawa when the
Basha pulled him off. He was weeping and kissing her bare
legs thinking she was dead. Although Sagawa was completely
unconscious, which was what happened when she went stiff
and fell, and turned as cold as a piece of metal, the Basha lifted
Sahm into the air. Then the flames roared and the house was
filled with the smell of flesh roasting on the spit.

Amma Fatima continued to come and go and sit next
to Al-Najdiyya, grinding coffee beans and cardamom while
the Basha sat on his terrace. Important guests would still pay
visits and he would roll out the red carpet for them and talk
about His Majesty who came to hunt at Anshas and Qaroun,
or Wadi Al-Rayyan. Amma Fatima would look after the girls,
keeping an eye on Hind as she leant her head over the veranda
while Sahla and the little servant girls played with dolls
made of straw and cotton. Then Amma Fatima retired to her
house and for a long time she never visited or came to say
to my mother: "May God have mercy on the souls of our
dear ones." Now when I pass her home many of her sons
don't know me. I used to go and visit her though and I'd
see her crooked body in its black Bedouin dress embroidered

in bright colours with a red cloth tied around her waist, and rubbed sage in her pocket. She had started to lean on a thick stick and as I walked up to her she would look at me through her narrow eyes and sing to the rhythm of my footsteps: "Sheikh Al-Arab's daughter, dressed in fine striped silk," or "Sheikh Al Arab's daughter, how sweet your tresses smell."

I would look at Amma Fatima, but it was Nawwar, who had long stopped carrying me and now walked beside me, leaving my steps to precede hers a little out of modesty, who would lead me over to greet the old lady. Amma Fatima had been so dear to Al-Najdiyya then Al-Najdiyya had died and I didn't know if Hind was still in the dark house or if she'd gone to join her.

Years later the adjoining mud houses of Clan Mizayna had turned into buildings of reinforced concrete with grocers' shops and ironmongers on the ground floor. When I walked past no one called out to me, but I could still smell the rubbed sage and the cardamom that was no longer in her pocket, and I would ask God to have mercy on the soul of Amma Fatima.

5

--

Inshirah is the one in Hind's photograph wearing the short dress and baggy trousers. She was a black woman, strapping and healthy with a voice that Al-Najdiyya could never quite manage to subdue. They say Jidd Munazi' bought her mother from a place called Wad Madani. He was on his way home with the caravans that bring gum and ostrich feathers and scented woods. A long line of men and women brought up the rear, their wrists bound to ropes that swung from the camels' backs. The hot sun beat down as young girls were forced to march on tired swollen feet across trackless sands, void of any sign save the skeletons of camels, hyenas and humans who had expired long ago on some journey along that same route. Every time they stopped at a trading post they would off-load some of their cargo and sell the goods for paltry prices, and by the time they reached the Red Sea their wares were much diminished. Jidd Munazi' brought back lots of slaves from the Upper Nile and settled them on his land at

the bottom of the high hill. People called them the slaves of
Clan Munazi'. Inshirah lived there with them, where Mubarak
the Slave built his house. Later he erected a spacious pavilion
for his guests and acquired a Land Rover, and whenever a circle
of visitors gathered round the coffee pot he would proudly
announce to all and sundry: "Kuwaitis," or "Saudis." The
guests would set off after him in more luxurious vehicles to
chase the gazelles of Ayla and Al-Alaqi. On these hunting
trips the slaves of Clan Munazi' became faithful guides. When
Amma Mizna visited them she didn't have the audacity to
talk to them like she had before, when she used to call them:
"Our dear friends and servants." But they still stood up the
moment they saw her and when she held out her hand they
would come up one after the other to kiss it, and address her
as they always had: "Our master's daughter."

Inshirah still lives there now. Whenever Muhra walks past,
Inshirah doesn't recognize her for she no longer remembers
anyone, not even her own grandchildren who play around the
house. Since the day they took her out of the dark house her
eyes have been filled with a sleepy redness, weary and exhausted,
unable to focus unless she squeezes them almost shut. The
children, who address Inshirah as: "*Ya* Jidda," eye Muhra
cautiously when she crosses the dirt track behind the gently
sloping hills. People say that in the past Inshirah used to
tie the dirty old belt, where the keys to the grain store and
the pantries hung, round her waist, but now her collar bone
protrudes from the neck of her dress, an indication of her
skinny, almost skeletal frame. The *shunnaf* hanging from
her nose has stretched the flesh and it dangles loosely against
her top lip. She has tied a cord round her head to support her
heavy earrings and it leaves a wide rut in her skin before it
passes under her headscarf, which she attaches to her hair
with coloured pins.

In her youth Inshirah was everywhere, always coming and going, making a terrible racket with her huge anklets and the jangling of the keys and her voice bawling at the servants: "Do this! Don't do that!" Al-Najdiyya had put her in charge of counting the sacks of flour, seeing to it that the rooms were properly cleaned and making sure the kitchens had all they needed. It was Inshirah who checked the eggs had hatched and the ducks had enough feed, and which animals' udders had dried out or filled up. And at the end of the day Inshirah would sit contentedly at her mistress's feet and massage them with mustard oil and warm water.

"Ma'am," she used to say, "we've filled a jug of gee," or "Ma'am, we've opened a pot of cheese," and "Ma'am, how many kilos shall we bake tonight?"

It was that very same Inshirah who was charged with taking Al-Najdiyya's gold far away from the prying eyes of the soldiers whenever they turned up. They would have in their hands lists of names and the Basha's land was turned into small holdings each no larger than two *feddans*. Then they built walls round them and dug irrigation ditches to water the land. Other soldiers carried off the horses, camels, ostriches and young gazelles and divided up the land which used to be called "The Bedouin Estate" into a chess board, leaving the gardens of Clan Al Basil completely empty; no birds of prey, no mares, no gazelles fenced in their pens. Al-Najdiyya gathered all the gold necklaces and ornaments that hung on her daughters' chests, and their thick braided anklets, and their brooches and pendants and wrapped them all up in a dirty old rag and tied it round Inshirah's waist so she could go and sit by the irrigation ditch under a tamarisk tree that spread its branches out over the water. Al-Najdiyya made Inshirah take her baby girl Nawwar with her too, to make her look even more inconspicuous. Inside the little one's tattered dress she hid some gold guineas wrapped up in a cloth. And as Inshirah hummed a lullaby to the little girl sat on her lap the soldiers would say to Al-Najdiyya: "Slaves'll sell you just like you sell them." But Inshirah would return in the evening bearing her cargo and there would not be a thing missing. And that's what she continued to do, every time an armoured car turned up.

There was a time when you could hear Inshirah's voice from the other side of the fields, and her vigorous movements echoed through the house. But then she stopped talking altogether. Some said it was the shock of losing Sahm, others a broken heart. She hadn't smelled the fire that caught in Sahm's clothes and burned the whole pavilion down with him inside it until it was too late. No one ever told her how the flames had burnt the body, or how the legs had been tied up. She wandered morosely from the bake house to the pantry to the threshing shed but she didn't say a word until they bound Hind by the legs and tied her to the bed. Then she said: "I will stay with my master's daughter until the end."

Inshirah carried Hind to the building at the end of the garden path, which was lined with lemon trees and old, tumbled-down pigeon towers. It was an old, two-roomed house made of mud and straw and filled with piles of rubbish and the remains of an old bed. I used to try and imagine what else was inside. In the ceiling of one of the rooms was a round opening between the wooden slats through which they lowered down the food basket and other items.

Inshirah, who is holding Hind in her lap in the picture, continued to hold her inside that closed house, in the room with the opening in the roof. There was a water pump there and Hind would sit under it every time her dress was soiled with urine or faeces. Inshirah worked the pump and the water poured over Hind's body which curled up into a wretched and submissive ball. The water that spilled onto the floor flowed down a little channel through a hole in the wall to drain out at the foot of the lemon trees. Through the opening in the roof the two women would know the beginning and end of the day, the seasons of orange blossom, the humming of mosquitoes in summer, the dripping of rain on the roof, and the smell of stagnant water around the trees. The windows of the two rooms had been filled in with silt and straw and were eerily quiet; not a sound was heard from within nor entered from without. Daylight alone came in through the opening in the roof. At the top of each room was a small aperture next to the wooden beams on the ceiling and they allowed the air to circulate a little. The mice knew about them, as did the cats and the little birds and some bats and spiders, but these holes let nothing else in. Hind would curl up on the bed and peer towards them. She would weep and succumbed to fits of sobbing and wailing, and scratch the walls with her fingernails. Inshirah's firm hands would hold her during these convulsions until they passed. Then she would lay Hind's head to rest in her lap as she recited spells and incantations and rebraided the locks of her hair (chains of gold Al-Najdiyya used to call them) into one long plait. After a while Hind would quieten down once again and wallow silently in the torment and anguish of her state.

Inshirah said that towards the end Hind was like a gentle breeze. She stopped slapping her cheeks and banging her head against the wall and focused all her senses on what was going on outside. She would put her ear against the wall to listen to the steady thud of the pestle as it pounded coffee beans or sniff the smell of roasting lamb. Sometimes she would say to herself: "They'll be in the kitchen now, lighting the fire under the large pans," or "Al-Najdiyya still keeps that box of snuff tucked inside the top of her *jallabiyya*." Through the opening in the roof she watched the constellation Gazelle Tracks, as the few scattered stars running across the sky came into view. She knew as they moved into this position that another year had passed, while she still fingered the walls and listened out for any sound, a mewing cat, a bird's wings flapping in the trees, new leaves falling at the stir of an autumn breeze. She could not see the wrinkles on her face or the white hairs that had encroached suddenly upon her parting. Inshirah saw them though, as she laid Hind's head in her lap to plait her hair, and sang:

> I've been patient so long,
> What good has it done?
> The door of hope is closed,
> All chance of salvation gone.

Hind increasingly succumbed to bouts of abject despair, and that brought on her crying fits again. Then she would stare grave and wide-eyed at unknown things that moved about in the darkness, certain that the door of hope was closed like the taciturn walls around her, and that even if she were to get out, an impregnable barrier of isolation would be set up around her. There was nothing to do but gaze into space. They did not know if she was even aware that she had a child sitting submissively in Sahla's lap, but they suspected that she sent out her spirit to search for her. They would say they had seen her kneading dough with them and that, when they looked round, a cat hissed and then ran away. Some of them saw her as she used to be, making the beds or drinking from the scented water on the edge of the terrace, then she would rub up against Sahla's legs and come out miaowing and clawing the carpets which were hung up for beating. And although they whispered to one another about the spirits of the living and the dead, every single one of them avoided mentioning her, or going to see her, even if only to peer through that small opening in the middle of the roof. For it seemed as if that would bring all kinds of pain to bear upon them. They simply made do with asking Nawwar: "Is your mother well, girl?" They never asked about Hind, and it was enough for Nawwar to tilt her head for them to be reassured.

This darkness into which she peered did not frighten her any more, nor did the dogs barking in distant fields. She sat huddled up in the fading light or the pitch black of night, piling up grains of sand on the floor of the room that they hadn't covered with wooden boards. They had left the earth for her to dig with her nails and make long furrows, like the intersecting lines she scratched on the unpannelled and unpainted walls. The soil was such that it turned to sand when she scratched it. Armies of ants had constructed barracks in it and crawled hither and thither between their holes. She did not try to count the days or to record their passing with marks. It was Inshirah who was able to associate definite signs with the hour and the seasons by the stars that passed over the opening in the roof and the smell of the orange blossom when it bloomed. Perhaps she waited for death but she did not attempt to bring it on. She had lost the ability to do anything except stare and she did not try to run away. She had surrendered completely. With her shoulders hunched over a pile of sand, she would gaze up at the tiny gap in the top of the wall or squat under the meagre portion of sky that rolled over the opening in the roof. She gave up her body to the night dew in a desperate attempt to inhale something other than the fetid air and the smell of stagnant water under the pump. Sores covered her legs from all that sitting on the floor but Inshirah was unable to cure them with onion skin and ashes. Each day new ulcers would appear weeping pus, and a hacking cough afflicted her. "Poor thing," they would say as they looked at her body and poured the last water of her death-ablution over it. As Hind neared the end they did not place "the little girl" who ran round Lamloum Basha's house in her lap, not even once, because she would not have remembered her. But then again, perhaps she did remember, often, as she put her ear against the hard deaf walls and picked out no sound save a distant hubbub which she would try to interpret. It was some commotion over a woman with short hair whose waves and curls resembled the hair of Layla Murad and Esmahan. She had a long nose and was called Sahla. They were sowing her a wedding dress with a low cut neck, so she could go to the same house that Hind had left.

"Your nose belongs to you even if it is crooked," Lamloum Basha was declaring, over the sobbing of his youngest daughter. "A girl will marry her cousin even if it is the last thing she wants. An Arab girl's like an obedient she-camel: the place you tether her, that's where she kneels, the place you lead her, that's where she goes."

When Sahla set off for Mutlig's house, carrying the baby girl who is in the photograph wearing a white crochet dress, no one said: "Poor thing" about her, because that was not how she wanted things to turn out. No longer the little girl who went to Minazi' Primary School carried on Nawwar's shoulders, Muhra now held the end of the thread in her hand. The photographs were blurred images, and it was up to her to fill in the details, as if there was a path she had to follow to the end, and a similar destiny she would be obliged to repeat. Hind came to her often, telling her to close the box, but she would not be swayed.

6

—-—

The frame that once was gilt had turned as pale as sand, more in keeping with the mood of the painting which her mother had taken with her, from Al-Najdiyya's house to her father's house, and then to the house in Al-Manyal. On each occasion she gave it pride of place in her sitting room. She would stare at it for hours, her eyes falling upon the row of men, the dancer swaying in front of them, and the camel train in the distance, disappearing over a vague watery horizon. At first Muhra thought that the thin young man who stayed for several months in the pavilion and painted the picture must have really meant something to Sahla. He called himself Sulayman, and spent many a summer's night sitting on the rug with Lamloum Basha chatting about Balqees and Solomon, who was able to hear the ants conversing with one another beneath his feet, and about his descendants in Abyssinia. At the end of every sentence Lamloum Basha would interrupt him to announce that Jidd Minazi' had been one of the first explorers to reach the source of the Nile, and that he understood exactly what the young man was saying, except that Balqees, Queen of Sheba, had lived in Yemen not Abyssinia. Sulayman, however, was somehow unable to give up this belief.

Sulayman, or Pierre, as he signed his work, would spend all day painting, locked in his room plying his colours until evening when he would dress like them in a white *thobe*, *igal* and thin white head cloth. His complexion was very fair despite the pimples on his face. He would sip coffee with them as he expounded his theory of reincarnation. He believed that an endless cycle of souls inhabited different living forms, such as human beings, tree branches or cats. He was convinced that his preoccupation with the Bedouin was in his soul, and that his soul might once have been incarnated in the body of an Arab filly, before it dwelled in the body of an equatorial monkey and then settled in his body. Next time round it might transmigrate into the bodies of beings he didn't even know existed. The Basha, obviously, thought him quite insane. They had met lots of crazy people like him passing through on their way here and there. One Jidd or another had come across white men looking for gold in the Laqaya Hills of the Eastern Delta, or emeralds in the mountains of Al-Bajja in the deep South. They told stories of one European who had worn an Arabian *qaftan* and wandered round from village to village. He had come with Bonaparte, and like Sulayman he depicted their *majlises* on huge canvases. He slept out in the open with them on camel hair and sheepskin. His name was Dinon and he joined Mahjoub Al-Kabir and Younis on many trips looking for new things to paint, such as the peasant women in front of their ovens, or weddings and circumcisions, or *moulids*.

All kinds of foreigners used to pass through in the days before Jidd Minazi' built his pavilion, which was designed by Baron Empain himself. The Baron used to hunt with them and often came up to Lake Qaroun, where the quails nested, or searched for mummies in Kom Ousheem or Nazlit Al-Nasara with his colleague, Dorvetti. The two would always end up with Jidd Minazi' as he prepared his camels to set off on trails that he had been the first to tread. Then he decided to build the pavilion, which was neither a goat-hair tent, nor a mud hut filled with smoke, but rather a tall house like those the English love to live in. It consisted of several rooms with wooden beams and mirrors that covered half the wall, curtains of silk and thick gabardine to keep the light out, and long stairways with wrought iron banisters. There was a room with Persian carpets, embroidered cushions and incense burners. The windows were covered with wire mesh to keep out mosquitoes and snakes, and there were large wooden wardrobes, and a wide veranda looking out over the stables at one end and the orange and lemon groves on the other. It was a wonderful structure, fit for guests such as Empain, De Lesseps, or Dorvetti. Later the pavilion would inspire the architectural style Al-Najdiyya chose for other halls and rooms. Hind's house was done in the same manner, but she only lived there for a while before she came back and they put her in a mud house next to the lemon trees and the dilapidated pigeon towers and closed up the windows.

Pierre, who had renamed himself Sulayman, was proud to be staying in the same place as Dorvetti. "That man was an explorer," he used to say, as if it were a great achievement. The Basha would retort that Jidd Minazi' was a great explorer too, just like Dorvetti. He would tell Pierre how the two men had mounted their horses and ridden out on long hunting trips. His Majesty had joined them on one occasion. They had travelled for days, eventually reaching Qous or Rayyan or Qaroun or the Emerald Mountains. Whenever they spotted a herd of gazelle, wild ass or antelope grazing peacefully, they would give chase. The animals would turn and bolt, leaving tracks in the sand like engravings. The hunters would follow them into stony riverbeds where the herds scattered, abandoning their young to the hunters while they hid among the rocks and boulders and observed the fate of their little ones as they were surrounded by salukis on all sides.

Dorvetti, who came to Jidd Minazi' looking for a pair of original Arab horses to send back to Vienna, and a pair of hawks trained to hunt gazelles, accompanied him to Sinnar and Al-Kababeesh Mountains and then to Barbar and Shindi. He was always on the look out for a pair of antelopes for the Emperor of Austria, ostrich feathers for the Duchess of Provence, equatorial insects for the Natural History Museum in London or a giraffe to enrich the royal collection of wild animals in Paris. Jidd Minazi' on the other hand was looking for the Golden Tributary. Calcified stones sparkled in its murky waters and they discovered after dissolving the outer layer that there was real gold in the shape of a stone. In reality it did not matter what Jidd Minazi' was looking for, because the two of them went on many trips together and always returned in the end to stretched out their legs in the pavilion of Clan Minazi', which was surrounded at that time by a huge wall just like a castle. Its floors were covered with Persian carpets and the smell of Mekkan incense mixed with the aroma of roasting meat and cups of coffee that were never empty.

Long afterwards the Basha planted camphor trees and tall poplars to enhance the seclusion between the pavilion and the house that the original fortification had provided. But the room where Pierre sat mixing his colours was just over that wall from the kitchen and the ovens where the young women hung out. In one place, some of the bricks had come away where the servant girls used to clamber up to see the red carpet being rolled out for strangers. Cars would pull up, bearing powder and shot and people with red foreign faces that the sun and the galloping up and down dry wadis would make even redder. Over that half broken-down wall the man who was to become my father came to chase the little servant girls. He lusted after Farhana's breasts and cornered Rawda on the straw in the sheep pen. The girls used to talk about it among themselves. Perhaps Hind heard them one night as they were whispering about virginity and the rites of the wedding night. On a Thursday night, when all the girls used to bathe to the smell of fire and steaming water and the sound of the pump, Inshirah stayed inside by the hearth. They would hang their clean clothes on the branches of the mulberry tree and sit on the straw combing their hair. He knew the time and made ready for it. He would lie in wait on top of the wall then jump down among the girls, splashing water on a naked body or the back of one who was rubbing her feet over the basin of soap suds. In the kitchen, Inshirah, who would be fast asleep in her chair, would raise her head at the racket and roar at the girls: "Get a move on, young lady! You've made me twist my neck with your antics. You, girl! Pour the water and be quick about it, may Allah shorten your life!"

As Mutlig climbed back over the wall, his scrambling feet would wear away some more of the brick work, which made the escapade easier each time, though no one noticed. From this it was possible to deduce that Hind had done the same and crossed over the wall to see the thin young man who called himself Sulayman, and spent time with him in the pavilion talking about monkeys and slaves from Sudan.

Sahm moved freely between the two worlds, from the pavilion to the house, and back again. He told Al-Najdiyya that Sulayman was painting slaves piled up naked on a ship; he said he had seen them in a place called Harar. He drew a sky full of storks and a desert where the bones of expired camels lay and hawks flew in the air, pulling at the tethers round their talons in a desperate attempt to break free. He

47

drew some fillies standing submissively in their stable. One had Hind's eyes. Sahm did not tell Al-Najdiyya that he had seen that picture in which Hind lay naked. Those who knew Hind's body, like Inshirah, kept it to themselves that the birthmark between the breasts really did belong to Hind, and the breasts that were like soft crimson roses were hers too. It was only in the picture though that she had silver anklets, like those of Inshirah, but they were linked with thick chains that hung down between her feet, and on her long hair was a string of jasmine running from her forehead to the end of the locks which were half hidden. Between her thighs he had painted the dark fur of a lynx and a face just like a cat's, although apart from the eyes, it looked like her pubic hair.

That was the cat they would see years later, meowing and clawing the carpets. They did not know how it got into the house through closed doors or how it sneaked past them to go back outside, but it had Hind's eyes and the same submissive nature, the same defiant streak of independence. Those who knew Hind said that she used to play records to learn how to dance the jive and do the twist. She would sit on her own trying to sing like Fathiyya Ahmed, and she would recite passages from *The Lady of the Camellias* in a trembling voice under the trees in the garden. Then her brother, who now lives in New Jersey, noticed what she was doing. He tore up the novel she had borrowed from Miss Angela, the headmaster's daughter, and punched Hind in the face. Her nose bled. After that she sat threading garlands of jasmine from the garden as she sang *My Love is so Tender*.

After Sulayman left they spotted a strap of giraffe skin round Hind's neck; on it hung an oval piece of stone with a round hole carved in the middle. It looked just like an ivory eye. It stayed on her neck, and no one removed it until Inshirah took it off, after she had poured water over Hind's body and anointed it with perfume as they wrapped her in towels and said: "Poor thing." Inshirah, who believed in all the magic spells, said that giraffes have knowledge of the supernatural, and all the priestesses in Addis Ababa and Sinnar use cords of giraffe skin to hold their charms and amulets. She also said that ivory has magical properties because it is an inanimate substance issuing from living flesh, and that the eye that hung around Hind's neck was for protection, just as ivory eyes protect the mummies and decomposing corpses in ancient tombs. Inshirah, who believed that the necklace was a charm signifying everlasting love, gave it to Sahla, who in her turn would place it in an old folder with some photographs and scraps of paper and clippings from the torn novel: *The Lady of the Camellias.*

Sahla took the folder to Mutlig's house with the painting of the caravan disappearing into the distance and the dancer and the row of men. She hung it in her room in front of the chair she used to sit on, so that she could see through the window on her right and look at the painting on the opposite wall. That was after the Basha had said:

"A girl will marry her cousin if it's the last thing she wants."

"The girl has other cousins," retorted Al-Najdiyya. "You don't have to give all your daughters to *him.*"

Those who knew Hind would relate how much she wept when she heard of Mutlig's exploits with Farhana and the other girls in the stables, and the tales they told about Fatima Al-Gurumiyya. But the Basha's response would always be the same:

"He's her father's brother's son; he's the first in line."

Hind's wedding dress was made for her by Madame Christine; it had a full skirt over many layered petticoats. They bought her a bottle of Le Soir lavender, and a pair of stiletto heels. On her wedding night she stood there among the torches held aloft by the slaves. Trays of henna edged with candles were carried twice round the yards and houses of the aunts and uncles. The dancer performed on the open land in front of the pavilion while the singer emerged from the line of men who clapped the rhythm with their hands. Bowing before her imploringly, he celebrated in his song the long she-camel neck of the beloved, her heels that shone like beacons, and her nose-ornament glistening like the crescent moon:

> Shining like shops in the Christian Quarter
> Your heels blazing beacons burning and bright,
> Rich ruby jewels on your cheeks gleam and twinkle,
> Fire on your forehead casts radiant light,
> Yours is the beauty of sunrise at dawn
> Lovely as the crescent moon on the twelfth night.

As the female dancer coyly reveals one eye, the excitement of the male dancers rises and their bodies slowly sway. She inclines her waist towards the singer of the verses, almost touching, then pulling away as she wards him off with her stick then once again softly bending her body back towards him. Al-Najdiyya and her female guests had to order the younger girls to attend to the bride rather than let their eyes wander over to the dance floor in front of the pavilion on the other side of the tumbledown wall. In the morning they put her on a howdah like her mother and her grandmother, even though the Basha had a motor car. There was only a large house and a wall separating Hind's new home from Al-Najdiyya's, so they walked behind the howdah still clapping their hands and singing love songs until they reached their destination. They had prepared her a room with wooden beams and mirrors, and a pale leaf-green bedspread while Al-Najdiyya had filled the dressing table drawers and the cupboards with alum, clove powder, rose oil, mint leaves and camphor and rubbed mastic in wooden boxes. Next to the bed they had placed scented oils with which they advised her to massage sensitive places, and to rub some on her lips as well, and to always keep the smell of mastic and bitter *liban* on her tongue. Then they left her with Fatima Al-Gurumiyya, knowing all too well what kind of woman Fatima was, as indeed did most of the men.

Al-Najdiyya used to relate how Fatima Al-Gurumiyya had come to the Bedouin estates with a little girl on her arm many years before. She had always been fair skinned and rather large in the sense of well-proportioned plumpness. Everyone used to remark how she'd had lots of husbands. The last one was Hilmy, the Upper Egyptian: skinny and ugly, he used to work in the flour mill. He would tip the grain into the opening on top of the machine and then stand by the transmission belt where the milled flour collected. Each woman would bend down to collect her share while he watched as their headscarves came undone, or drops of sweat trickled down their cleavages. Fatima Al-Gurumiyya always wore *jallabiyyas* that revealed her outrageously ample breasts, always topped by a necklace of cheap emerald beads that blended with the dark crimson colour of her lipstick and her slightly yellowing teeth. She was still attractive though, and Hilmy must have enjoyed the view because he married her.

Fatima Al-Gurumiyya always paid a visit to the bride's house the night before a wedding. The young woman would be standing there naked as her hair was removed. Fatima Al-Gurumiyya would rub crushed alum and mastic under the bride's armpits, check her private parts and pluck any residual hairs to make sure the skin was as smooth and soft as that of a new-born babe. She would trim the eyebrows with thread and scrub the body. Then she would have a look at the bride's underwear and give her opinion on this negligee or that, and offer advice as to whether it would be better to wear the hair down or tie it back with pins, or straighten it with oil and cream. The more conservative houses would suffice themselves with having her bring a red satin nightdress, and seek her opinion on such matters as padding out the bra with cotton wool, or tying in the stomach with belts especially after child birth. The older women would ask her about other things such as which side it was better to lie on when doing you know what, or lifting up the legs, or the most erotic sounds to make. Fatima Al-Gurumiyya would sprinkle some tobacco into a cigarette paper and roll herself a smoke, then raise her eyebrows as she laughed her raunchy laugh and made lewd gestures with her hands.

Madame Christine sewed Hind's clothes, and Miss Angela went all the way into town to buy her a selection of night dresses by Gautinio, a powder case and some lipstick. Before the wedding she spent ages tying Hind's long hair up over her veil. The girls strewed camphor and basil leaves under Hind's feet so her new life would be green and sweet smelling. Then they left her to Fatima Al-Gurumiyya. She carried in a lamp for Hind and hung it over the bed. She placed Hind's head in her lap and grabbed her firmly by the arms. Then she hooked her feet round Hind's thighs to spread them wide open so Mutlig could poke a couple of jabs with his finger. Crimson drops dripped onto the pale green cloth while Hind stifled her scream. Having completed the ritual, Mutlig and Fatima Al-Gurumiyya emerged from the room together and left Hind inside to swallow her tears as she listened to the two of them laughing and smelled their tobacco in the distance.

On the veranda with its wood and wrought iron railings there is a door leading into the guestroom, another door into the house, and Hind's bedroom window. Today the rectangular floor of the veranda has dark tiles, the colour of earth, but perhaps they were a different colour in those days. That is where Hind used to stand and look out at the lamps hanging in a huge mulberry tree to light up the yard. In the distance she could see the lights of Al-Najdiyya's house, and the veranda where the old woman sat taking snuff up her nostrils and sneezing, and ordering the servants to bring pots of rice and pancakes with fresh cream to her daughter who was now far away, the property of another man. Between the two houses were only the birds and emptiness, some old mud buildings and nocturnal silence. Hind used to stand there for ages waiting for him to return from Fatima Al-Gurumiyya's house. He would have to support himself against the wall, his clothes reeking of smoke and strange fragrances on his breath: opium or hashish, or other things she didn't know. While she sat up waiting for him she may have smelled of those powders they had filled her drawers with. In any case the servants definitely said that he was sleeping at the house of Fatima Al-Gurumiyya and that Hind wouldn't stop crying. A few nights later Hind walked into the house of Al-Najdiyya, and made her swear on the lives of the dear departed that she wouldn't make her go back. She promised that she would live as a servant in her father's house.

"Please don't send me back to him," she pleaded. "I'll die if you send me back."

Al-Najdiyya scolded her and said she was behaving like a spoilt little girl. She told her that everything was up to the woman and she should make more effort with him because all men behave rashly and then come to their senses.

So Hind went back to her veranda, desperately alone, to face the night-time dew with more tears. She degenerated into stony silence and fits of sobbing. She would stare blankly into space for days at a time, leave her urine and faeces to stain her clothes, and reject any attempt to clean her up or feed her. Mutlig led her back to Al-Najdiyya's house propped up by the servant girls and Al-Najdiyya poured cold water over her head and tugged her plaits in an attempt to bring her to her senses.

"You'll do what your family says," she said, "even if it breaks your back. You'll go back to him, you'll go back! You can walk up and down but you'll go back. He's your father's brother's son and you'll stay in his house till the day you die."

Hind looked at her and burst into bitter tears. They took her back to her house a few days later with crates of mangoes, some freshly slaughtered meat and a few pieces of soap. They burnt incense in every room then they left her there and went back to Al-Najdiyya's.

She did not cry after that. Even so, the servants had to go out and fetch her when she went out at night and stood stark naked in a stupor under the stars. When she came round she wouldn't remember a thing. One night she walked all the way to Al-Najdiyya's house in that state and stood in front of Lamloum Basha when he opened the door to her continuous knocking. He yelled at the servants to cover her in the first sheet they could find. Her belly was swollen a little and that same blank look of astonishment was in her eyes. They gathered round her in disbelief. She could not understand why they were looking at her with such concern and apprehension. She did not weep or scream or collapse on the floor in convulsions like Sagawa but they tied her legs and arms, put her on the bed and locked the door. When the swelling in her belly became flesh and blood, they led her away to the dark house where they undid her bonds and closed up the windows and doors. There, through the opening in the roof through which they lowered the baskets, Hind watched as the fleeing gazelle left behind her little newborn child, that had not learned how to run, in the desolate pitch-black sky.

7

—-—

There is no wedding photograph of Sahla with a garland of jasmine or a diamond tiara. All she got was a lilac table cloth and curtains the same colour. They didn't change anything about the room where Hind had lived before her, and I don't know whether Fatima Al-Gurumiyya went in with her too or not. In photographs she always looked the same: sitting on a chair, just as thin as she is now. She inherited her tall figure, solemn nose and taut skin from her father. Al-Najdiyya used to say she had a neck like a she-camel; that distinguished neck that none of her sisters had, and her eyes were dark and deep. Al-Najdiyya had bequeathed her neither fairness nor ruddiness and her hair did not fall over her shoulders in long luxuriant tresses like Hind's or Sagawa's, but was rather short, thick and jet black. I remember seeing her rolling her fringe around old stockings stuffed with cotton wool in the shape of small cylinders to act as rollers so that it dropped in curls over her eyebrows. She had her parting on the right, and she put in more stuffed stocking at the back to turn it under and add waves. She was mad about the hair styles of Layla Murad and Esmahan.

In one photograph Sahla is wearing a sleeveless red dress with flowers the colour of jasmine. It has a low neck line and reveals her arms, and comes down to just below the knee where it is held out by a ruffled petticoat. She is wearing a string of white pearls around her long full neck. Perched on her knees is a baby girl, soft and white like cotton wool, dressed in a white knitted dress. Sahla is holding the child elegantly and with great poise and her legs are held demurely together. It seems from the photograph as if she has only ever been the woman with the little girl on her lap, and that all I have ever done is sit there on that lap, in the room with lilac curtains. In the morning she would sit by her bed in a deep armchair facing the window that looked out onto the vines and mulberry trees. I would be standing next to her when Mutlig came in, his intuition having informed him that she had awoken and put on the sky-blue dressing gown that made her more graceful and distinguished, with her hair tied back to reveal her long neck and her deep, wide eyes. After making sure she had heard his knock, he would enter the room, bend over his daughter, and kiss her cheek as he waved his hand in the air in front of her. "Is my cousin well?" Muhra would hear him say or "Does my cousin want anything?" And when Sahla sat on the terrace doing her embroidery, in the mornings if it was winter, or at night if it was summer, he would park his back against the wall, stretch out his legs on the floor and talk about fillies and falcons, or planting new palm trees in the yard, or an upcoming hunting trip. He never spoke to Sahla directly. It was as if he were talking to himself, and Muhra had to be there so he could say:

"Princess, your Uncle Mubarak says that Jabal Ataqa is still full of birds of prey. Hawks love remote places. When a free bird crosses the Red Sea, it alights exhausted on the first hill." After a short pause he would continue: "On our last trip your Uncle Mubarak released his hawk, Charger, behind a flock of bustards. Have you ever tasted bustard, sweetheart? The next trip I'll snare one for you; the shotgun kills it outright. Anyway my dear, your Uncle Mubarak says to the hawk: 'Go and see to your work, Charger!' Many's the time I've said to your Uncle Mubarak: 'Your hawk's no good,' and he wouldn't believe me. Imagine, Princess, the hawk comes down on the bustards from behind. Now, a bustard, when it sees a hawk behind it, spits out a liquid just like glue and the hawk's wing feathers stick together so it can't move and it falls out of the air. Your Uncle Mubarak calls out: 'Charger!' and just at that moment the bird falls from the sky with a pile of gluey gob on its back. Well, your father laughed till he almost choked. That night we had to eat the pigeons we'd taken out as bait. I said to your Uncle Mubarak: 'If we had a Singari falcon among our birds, or a red Kuhiyya, I would have been Sheikh of the Arabs long ago.' Do you know, Princess, Prince Lubad will pay fifty thousand for a Kuhiyya, for a single bird. By Allah, if the Good Lord gave your father a Kuhiyya and a falcon he would have become Sheikh Al-Arab. Have you ever tasted bustard, sweetheart? Its meat is white, just like turkey. In your grandfather the Basha's house there was a pen full of bustards. He used to rear them like we rear pigeons. May Allah have mercy on your grandfathers, cousin. May Allah have mercy on our dear departed ones."

Only when he finished speaking did it become apparent that he was trying to address the woman in the sky-blue dressing gown. She understood this perfectly well but she just didn't seem interested. And as he conducted his deals with the short peasant women who put their stamp and finger print on the deed and gave him the bank notes as he sold them another plot, she would grimace disapprovingly. He would attempt to evade her eyes by sitting the little girl on his lap and giving a rendition of his favourite song:

> If a man's money flits through his fingers
> Little can he do to change his lot.
> But a noble spirit's like gold, once broken
> The Lord recasts it in the smelting pot.

Lots of aunts and cousins came to sit on Al-Najdiyya's terrace with little children running around them. They poured cups of coffee and talked about Sahla; when would God compensate her with a child, they wondered. Sahla would watch Muhra as she played noisily with the other youngsters and say: "He's already done it." She wanted nothing more in her life than Muhra. When Muhra grew a little older and sat some distance apart from them, she would hear everything they said through the open window. She started to notice more direct questions about Mutlig sleeping in his tent, and not spending the night in Sahla's room. Sahla would answer softly: "Everyone sleeps on the side they find most comfortable." Given her reluctance to elaborate they were unable to surmise whether he slept in her room some nights or not. Later, when Muhra had managed to work these things out for herself, she discovered that he did not even dare look Sahla in the face. In fact, whenever he wanted to be next to her, she had to sit between them so that he could talk about his saluki which he had trained to catch jerboas; or describe how his party had lost their way on their last trip, and if it had not been for Abu Shreek Al-Iyadi, a former caravan guide who found his way by the stars, they would have perished. He seemed like a child seeking its mother's attention. Sahla would focus her gaze on something in the distance and nod her head in agreement, or she would watch Muhra's antics as if her daughter was the only thing that concerned her. She was obstinate and proud like a she-camel; still, silent and uninterested.

Jidda Fatima sprinkled water over Sahla so the nightmares would go away and Allah would calm her mind, and the ghosts that haunted her, those spirits from the underworld that kept her awake at night, would disappear. "Poor thing, daughter of the dear departed," Jidda Fatima would say. Perhaps all she really wanted to tell Sahla was that Mutlig no longer spent any time in the house of Al-Gurumiyya, and that now he might prove to be a good husband, but Sahla did not give the impression she was listening. Even Al-Najdiyya herself, in the face of her youngest daughter's reticence, did not know if Sahla was still a virgin and whether Mutlig had actually done the business. He would spend a long time away from us, but then the desire to come and sit by her side would suddenly seize him. He would come to contemplate the long neck and the penetrating eyes. He would sit Muhra in his lap, and stroke her hair, now it had grown a little longer.

"Princess," he'd say, "your filly has filled out and if her son is black like her, he will be the most noble horse of all the Arabs."

And he might spend hours telling her riddles:

> Keen-eyed o'er the waves a heaving
> Towards yon empty mountains weaving.
> No man can snatch him from the nest
> Nor mighty lord take the things which therein rest.

"A gazelle!" she'd shout, while his fingers stroked her hair.

He'd laugh: "And do gazelles cross the waves and live in the mountains, Arabian Princess?"

"A filly?"

"And do fillies hide in nests, Princess?"

"A hawk?"

"Correct, my little gazelle. The hawk crosses the waves and comes from lands of ice to alight on our desolate mountains. Do you know, my darling, why no lord, prince or king can obtain what is in his nest?"

Muhra would crouch in his lap asking for more:

"Because the hawk is a noble bird and does not eat from anyone's leftovers," he'd continue. "You have to leave him the bird in his talons so he can take the first bite from it. Then he will leave it for you."

Then Mutlig would lift her up onto his back and carry her to his tent where Amma Mizna sat boiling coffee and baking him bread in the ashes. She'd take Muhra from his arms and sing to her:

> With the eyes of a hovering hawk you gaze around
> And weak-willed folk like us shall in their glare be bound.

Amma Mizna was forever comparing Muhra to a hawk, and her dark eyes to those of a filly or a desert antelope. She never spoke to Sahla at all, or even entered the house. She just sat next to Mutlig, lit his fire, and gave him butter milk to drink. She used to ride down from Al-Alawaya, where she lived all on her own, on a donkey with saddle bags and a thick stick in her hand. Her saddle bags would be full of wheat bread, hard cheese and butter milk, and other kinds of food Muhra didn't even recognise. Amma Mizna went about in a black dress tied at the waist with a belt of red beads and the gold on her bosom hung down to her waist. When she crossed the roads that had become full of Gharabwa, Baramwa and Palestinians, and migrants and peasants of every description – people she could no longer address as "our dear ones and our servants," they would all stare at her in amazement. Only the old folk would say to her: "Please come in, mistress," until their children scolded them and reminded them that each man was his own master these days.

As Mutlig grew a little older, and Muhra grew older too, the three of them would sit on the balcony of the old house overlooking the boats on the Nile. The walls had faded and the picture frames that held the images of Lamloum Al-Basil, Pierre Kamm, Hind, Inshirah, and all the others, had lost their lustre. They looked like pathetic relics in need of major restoration, like the bathrooms from which issued lusty cockroaches and swarms of ants, and the furniture rendered threadbare by the passage of long years. There was nothing there except the river and the boats. Amid the marble buildings that hemmed in the house, the balcony's iron railing edged with wood looked almost as miserable and dejected as the three of us sitting there on bamboo chairs that had turned a dark and dusty colour.

He came only to check on his wife and daughter.

"Is my cousin well?" he would announce. And to Muhra he would say: "My Lady, would you take this eye or that?"

He looked much weaker and clearly longed to tell her of his travels to distant lands with Prince Lubad. She would help him lift the glass of tea in his trembling hand.

"Ah Princess," he would begin, "just one Singari peregrine, and your father would have become Sheikh of the Bedouin." She would pass him his tobacco case too: he was always forgetting where he put it. There was always a cigarette dangling from his mouth and his coughing fits were interspersed with the spitting up of painful stuff from deep inside his chest. Before leaving he would notice the grey hair she hadn't tinted with henna. She wore a knitted bonnet but had let a single white lock fall across her forehead. Time had left lines on her slender neck, making her somehow more alluring and refined, just as the modest dark clothes she now wore had made her more dignified.

8

—◦—

Fear not, my darling, that my love for you will die.
It abides beneath my lashes, dearer to me than my eye.

Father is wearing a white *thobe* and an *igal*, and he has
folded his white head cloth up over his head on either
side. He is leaning on his elbow and singing. In his mouth
burns a cigarette. His palm is turned inward and his hand
faces the camera. On it is perched a bird of prey. He always
called it Al-Hurr, meaning "the free one." Whenever he said
"Al-Hurr" we didn't know if he was referring to the breed as a
whole, or if that was its name: Al-Hurr. He trained it to sit on
his forearm when he bent his elbow and it flew above him
and landed on his shoulder when he walked. It would land
and take off again and then return to him. He always sat
with the goat-hair tent behind him and the sandy open space
in front. He was keen to keep it that way; open sand without

plants or trees, an empty space surrounded by walls that with the passing of time had crumbled and become less imposing. Muhra hung the photograph opposite her desk in an old frame the colour of the sandy emptiness that she loves. Whenever Sahla came into the room she would try to avoid looking at the wall that confronted her with his picture. She knew her eyes were running away and they would fail her time and again as they slunk back to inspect the cigarette in his mouth, Al-Hurr on his arm, and the ring that he had never removed still clearly visible on his finger. He would leave the tent and come to sit by Sahla's side on the balcony, claiming all the while he had come to sing songs to me so that I would become a true daughter of the Arabs:

> Fear not, my darling, that my love for you will die.
> It abides beneath my lashes, dearer to me than my eye.

Or

> Dear distant beloved, lonely and true,
> My heart evenings with me but sleeps only with you.

Muhra nodded her head to the song as he did, but she felt a pain in the pit of her stomach as Sahla turned her face away to contemplate the sky or the garden path, nonchalantly cracking her fingers as he strove to reach her through the cipher of his songs.

He wiped away his saliva with the edge of his sleeve; he leaned on his stick, and then took to his bed. The cough that occupied the gaps between his sentences now threatened to stifle his breath. Sahla had finally taken down the goat-hair tent and opened up for him the room with lilac curtains and the door leading out onto the veranda with wrought iron railings and wooden handrails. She planted basil round the edges and let the ivy drop down over the old wooden posts scorched by the sun. She opened the window opposite his bed, and a host of sparrows were chirping. He gazed at the sky and birds flying in the distance and started to reminisce:

He is reclining on a carpet in a spacious hall. There is a line of salt blocks for the birds. Fifteen birds of prey perch on the blocks; the salt prevents fungus spreading between their claws. He turns his cigarette in his mouth as he inspects them; three pure white falcons the Prince has brought from Canada. He checks the talons and the eye sockets to determine their age: they are all in their first year. The air conditioning which thrusts out cold air alleviates the scorching heat that emanates from the desert floor. On the other side of the room are five Nidawis, crimson red with light coloured spots splashed like dewdrops on their backs. He shakes his hand which juts out through the smoke:

"The Nidawis are vicious," he tells the men around him, "and this bald Nidawi is the most vicious of all."

The black Singari hawk which the prince loves to look at, stands alone. Mutlig tells them it is rare, a pure jet black Kuhiyya. The rest of the hawks are off to one side.

"The hawk is braver," he goes on, "but falcons are more intelligent. They get to know their owner and understand him simply by looking at him."

He leans back against the wall to take in all the birds, and sits there repairing snares with horse-hair, singing little songs to himself about eyes, talons and beaks. All the birds wear a thick leather hood over their eyes to prevent vision, and they are kept hungry and exhausted so they will better respond to him when he is training them. He raises his voice so they will become familiar with his intonation. He is passionate about poetry and has committed vast amounts to memory, just as he is passionate about the scene of which he is now a part. He gives the birds names he likes, all beginning with the consonant *seen*, that painful letter which is the first letter of Sahla, a distant and unbending name. He calls them Saad, Saba, and Sahm Saree' (which means "Swift Arrow"), and Sard, and Sind. Each bird knows the letters of its own name. As he pronounces the name he places a live pigeon in front of the Nidawi. Wings trussed up, the victim hops about in a futile attempt to escape the deadly blows and its own slaughter. Between the head and body the sharp beak plunges in and razor claws tear the feathers from the sides and open up the breast for that strip of flesh which is all it will eat of its prey. This, he says, is genuine Al-Hurr, "Free One," that will eat only live flesh; even if hunger has brought it close to death it will never be content with a corpse. After that he allows the hawk the pleasure of tearing off the pigeon's wings, and ties the legs with a piece of twine to the block. The Nidawi claws the body with its talons and tears away the flesh. Then it returns to perch proudly on its block. He sings to it:

Afraid of Al-Hurr, killer unhooded
Nidawi, dyed red, feathers all bloodied
He'll show you no quarter this falcon
Trained true by his master's own wisdom,
He catches the fearless and weak
And vermilion drips from his beak.

Mutlig savours the words as they leave his mouth and he repeats the songs again and again so that each hawk knows he is encouraging it. With the passion of a lover he sings to them.

He spends the long desert nights in that sandy wilderness where no one treads save a few Indian and Asian servants. He watches the villas and palaces of the princes in the distance, where headlights flicker and powerful cars bound up and down the road and the din never ceases. Then he peers into the mountain darkness beyond the dunes of sand that stretch as far as the eye can see.

"*Ya* Utayr," he says to the young Sudanese man who accompanies him when he is training the birds, "my Grandfather Al-Shafei, may Allah have mercy on our dear departed ones, had a hawk called Al-Qannou'. It would swoop down on its prey, finish it off and drink just a few drops of its blood. It would not even scratch the chest at all. My grandfather, may Allah rest his soul, would toss it its share as it perched on its block. Twelve years it lived with him until a sore appeared on its foot between its talons. They say that the pus ate away at the bones and damaged them. The bird grew old in just a few days and the ulcer on its leg became the size of a lemon. We found it one morning, a pile of feathers and as stiff as a board."

Utayr shakes his head and peers at a light in the distance: "The prince is back," he says. Mutlig continues smoking his cigarette and moving from one grandfather to another. He turns to look at the dark youth.

"My grandfather Minazi', may Allah rest his soul, traveled to your country many times," he says. "Do you know Wad Madani, *Ya* Utayr? That's where he got the mother of the slave woman who grew up in our house. She was called Inshirah."

Utayr, who used to talk to him about the cars piled up behind the palace, eaten away by rust or lack of use, tells him that he does not know Wad Madani, or Inshirah, or any of his grandfathers. He has come here to earn a bit of money, not to study someone else's family tree. Mutlig swallows the bitter coffee in one gulp.

"There's the smell of a fox about you, slave," he says to the young man.

Utayr rises to his feet and moves away to watch the buildings and cars. He leaves Mutlig alone to the desert night, eyeing the creatures that squat proudly atop their blocks like scarecrows planted there to frighten him.

During the day the hall is transformed into a circus. Mutlig flies the hawks one by one, calling each bird by its name:

"Sind, *Ya* Sind, can you see that pigeon? Fetch it, *Ya* Sind!" The bird takes off but instead of heading for its prey, it tries to escape and bumps into the ceiling. He pulls the jess that is still tied around its leg.

"*Ya* Sind," he continues, "you are a bad boy. Nothing to eat for you. Look at Saba while he fetches it. Saba, *Ya* Saba. You're cleverer than your friend. Fetch it."

The Singariyya is especially difficult. Every time she sees the light and feels the jess loosened around her leg, she collides with the wall.

"She's a stupid bird," he tells the prince, who has come with his entourage of many men to inspect his goods and see them training. "She's broken a fore-feather on the wing. I've been setting the break for the last few days, fixing it with gum and binding it with thread but she's a foolish one. She hasn't responded to the training so far."

The Prince shakes his head and says that he loves looking at her. "The stubborn she-camel, the stubborn filly and the stubborn hawk, each one captivates her lover's mind," he says.

The entourage laughs and the prince shakes his head.

"Even though her feather is set with gum and thread she still stands there all proud, haughty and remote. What did you call her?" he asks.

Mutlig smiles: "Sahla," he answers, "I called her Sahla."

The gazelles are on the gallop. Herds shimmering spectre-like in the distance. Courses of black rock eroded by the water that flows from springs high up in the mountains cut down into the wadi and wet pebbles glisten on the ground below. From the helicopter the surface of the wadi slumbers in the twilight. Mutlig chooses a platform of rock to their right and they land. A number of Indians and Asians scurry over the outcrop inspecting the ground for snake tracks. They say the place is called "Wadi Hyena." There is nothing in the emptiness save a few *ghardag* trees, and thorny bushes, which they set on fire to chase away the lizards. Thick smoke rises into the sky. Then they spread out carpets and put up air-conditioned tents and water coolers. Once the barbecue has been set up they take freshly slaughtered meat out of the cool boxes. The smell of cooking blends with the scent of cardamom and roasted coffee beans. When they have eaten they check over the equipment on the helicopter: the radar and the cameras that will film every scene so they can watch it again and again. The prince leans back and looks through his binoculars, surveying the low hills the herds must traverse if they are to reach the water. The vast plain dotted with clumps of grass stretches out before him. Mutlig goes and stands on the highest hill, takes his birds out of their cages and removes their hoods. The hawks head out in consecutive groups of three as he has trained them. On soaring wings they speed towards the herds that gallop ahead of them, searching desperately for high crevices where they can leave their young, who are confused by the beating hawk wings in their eyes. Each group of three rounds on a young gazelle, goading it with their wings in a series of vicious assaults, one flying high above the animal's head, leaving the second space to flap its wings in its eyes, while the third plunges its talons in above the forehead. The salukis unleashed in the birds' wake tug at the slender legs as they struggle to get away, and the gazelle falls exhausted to the ground, still alive. Once the prey has been stretched out and trussed at the legs, the Land Rovers pull up and the animals are slung into the back of the pick up. The flock that just a little while before was basking in the crimson light of the setting sun has left behind nine young gazelles piled in the back of the vehicles now returning to camp.

The hawks return. Each perches proudly on its salt block, contentedly chewing a piece of flesh from the breast of one of the pigeons that have been released to celebrate the bounty of the hunt and as a reward for their valour in the fray. His chest is filled with smoke and the exaltation of victory. He is gasping for breath and leans back against the wall of the tent, watching the videos of the chase as they play again and again to the applause of the prince and his companions. He listens happily to their comments:

"That yellow falcon shines like a gold guinea."

"Allah, what a hunter Al-Hurr is! The red one is a real pure bred."

"But the Free can live as long as fifteen years."

"Some birds can hunt for years but Al-Qannas, 'the Gazelle Chaser' can only hunt while he's in prime condition, a year or two old."

Mutlig wants to tell them that his grandfather Minazi' had a Free One named Al-Qannou' that lived for eleven years, but he decides not to. He just wheezes and looks at the black Singariyya in its jess, the hood over its eyes and the fore feathers he has set. The bird stands motionless. When they fly her she circles in the sky, and flaps her wings when they tug her jess.

"That one," they all say, "cannot be released or led. She's stubborn. Nought will turn her head save hunger."

It may have been at such moments that he longed to sit by her side and say to her: "My uncle's daughter, just like a bird of prey that beguiles the mind," but she was far away, and he was there alone. From time to time the Prince would come to Mutlig and ask:

"This killer that tears the gazelle's face with its talons, what shall I call him cousin?"

Sometimes Mutlig answers him "Saad," sometimes "Sarw," or "Saud." He gently strokes the broken feather with his finger, mindful of the claws with which the bird attacks any creature that approaches it in its unending darkness.

How can he keep up this pretence? How can he stand there on the hill as the prince calls out to him: "Bring your hawks, cousin!" The hawks have come to know his wrist and perch obediently awaiting a signal from his hand. He has chosen their names. They are in his dreams. They hover around him like young boys sprung from his own loins, his army which he commands and whose recent battles he has directed, to prove he is a true Arab huntsman. How can he not keep it up, when only minutes before he has given each bird a name according to the qualities he has observed in it.

"Saad is the most vicious, tearing with his talons, not leaving his prey until the marks of his assault are visible upon its hide. Surour is more intelligent; with one stroke to a certain spot he spills the blood of his victim but only licks up a single drop. In one fell swoop he takes the prey in a fatal embrace of talons and beak."

He has no choice but to keep it up. Now he stands there just to say the name of the bird and lift off its hood while the Prince releases it into the air.

"How much did we pay for this one?" he asks Utayr. The numbers that spring meaninglessly forth interest no one but Utayr. He is always leaning his back against a wall and telling himself that if he possessed even the rusty hulk of one of their abandoned cars he would be the richest man in his village. If he owned that white falcon he would enjoy absolute unchallenged authority. But his reflections come to an abrupt end as the Prince says: "The camels in the Valley of Al-Ajjaj are abundant." Nobody knows whether he is talking about his money or the birds in the sky.

When the game is over the birds, who a moment before were prisoners awaiting a signal from Mutlig's wrist, are hovering on the overcast horizon. They soar and circle and swoop down over the tents. "It is the bait that breaks them in," says the Prince with a laugh.

The birds, which Mutlig still calls Al-Hurr, lose themselves in the vastness of the sky. They have grown used to trussed-up pigeons beneath their feet, and standing on pegs waiting to obey a sign from their master. They hover high up in the azure void then swoop down low to scan the wadi that is now without camels or herds of gazelle: a wilderness deserted save for a few Land Rovers and some tents filled with laughter.

The Singariyya alone he keeps tied to her perch, agitated by the beating of wings around her, broken spirited, her eyes veiled.

"That dusky black one," the Prince says, "if I set her free, she will not return. Free-spirited women and free-spirited hawks are more stubborn than a granite mountain."

He laughs as if he relishes her abject state the same way he does the smell of grilled meat or the sound of the salukis barking in the darkness. The birds are still unable to do anything except circle in the sky above the tent. The prince tears off a piece of meat and throws it to his dogs.

"A dog barking for you," he says, "is better than a dog barking at you."

The men around him agree, confident that he will gather in all the birds like a turtledove gathers grains of wheat. All he has to do is release a brood of pigeons fitted with snares at the crack of dawn. They had been laughing, but in the dawn mist their laughter is silenced as the pigeons fly off with traps on their wings that resemble a net woven from threads of hair from a filly's tail, slippery and strong. The hungry hawks thrust their claws into the snare and are brought to the ground. They are returned to their cages, proof once again that even a free bird can be hooked by bait.

After that Mutlig no longer bothers to tell them about his grandfather Al-Shafei who would kindle his fires for passers by, claiming proudly that neither drought nor downpour would extinguish the fire of Clan Al-Shafei. Instead he recites verses about the generous and the mean, about the wind as it swirls, and drought which smites the land and casts free men into the country of strangers. He says things unconnected but they are totally captivated by his rhetoric:

> The earth is wide enough for a generous man to roam,
> But for him who fears insult, 't were better to head home.
> Nought in the world shall entrap you, though this I do advise,
> Travel willingly or in dread, so long as you are wise.

They nod their heads at the way he intones the words, testimony to his remarkable eloquence. Then he came home. He had been on the move a long time but never arrived anywhere.

At last he sleeps in the bed behind the drawn lilac curtains, dreaming of a headstrong Singariyya floating on the wing he had set after she broke her fore feathers. He no longer dreams of a pure white Olabi saker which he could sell for quarter of a million and become Sheikh of the Arabs. All he does is say:

> Money's a bane to a man with no breeding,
> As it moves through folk's fingers, their status not heeding,

But

> The rich man thinks he's noble and stands on solid ground
> But weak is his foundation: add another floor and
> the building tumbles down.

Amma Mizna, seated at his feet, is the only one to offer an explanation: money can raise the status of a lowborn man because it circulates among people, one day with you, one day with someone else. But the foundation that holds up a building is more important, for a decent origin and good breeding are the foundation of everything.

Sahla doesn't comment. Mutlig watches as her hand approaches to put the food in his mouth. He raises himself up with his wheezing chest, but he does not have the strength to gaze into those captivating eyes.

"My uncle's daughter has done so much for me," he says.

"It's nothing," she replies shaking her head, "as long as you will be well."

She says it in a forgiving almost affectionate tone that restores his eloquence and he recites another verse for me to hear:

> I have squandered my life waiting for a promise from her
> I have run a race with Time yet he remains fresh
> as I gasp for air.

This time I would not need Amma Mizna to shake her nose ornament and explain. Sahla slowly removes her hand from his trembling hand and walks out of the room. Amma Mizna takes off her sandals and spreads out her sheepskin rug on the floor. She sits opposite his bed resting her head against the wall and contemplates his pale face as he chases the phantom of a stubborn Singariyya with verses of poetry. He always makes great effort to attribute them to their authors: this one is by Majnoun Layla, and that by Majnoun Lubna, and this is a traditional Bedouin lay. Whenever she leans over him with the tablets he lets out a painful sigh and says:

"Allah knows the spirit will perish despairing of you, but I live in hope."

The fine wrinkles beneath Sahla's eyes become more pronounced. The muscles surrounding her mouth twitch and her smile becomes weaker and more feeble. In the room where the pictures hang she may burst into tears as the oxygen tubes pass through his mouth into lungs riddled with smoke and pain. He gasps a last breath of air and then flies off with his birds of prey, soaring behind the unbreakable Singariyya. Far away he passes and at last Sahla, daughter of Al-Basil, can weep freely. Now she is sadder and more serene when she looks at the photograph of him reclining with the cigarette in his mouth and Al-Hurr perched on his wrist. On his finger is the ring which she will put on her own finger as she opens the door of my room and finds herself facing the picture opposite the desk. She turns away, and closes her eyes while her breathing returns to normal.

9

——

Muhra, daughter of clan Al-Shafei, has now inherited two houses: one in Manyal Al-Roda where nobody lives any more, the other looking out over a canal filled with sand that used to be called the estate of Clan Minazi'. She has also inherited an old building facing her grandfather's house known as the pavilion. It is built of brick and polished wooden panels and the mirrors on its walls reflect only greying twilight. She goes to have a look at the room that faces the stable from one direction and the mango garden from the other. They tell her that Pierre, who called himself Sulayman, used to live in it. Still standing against the narrow balcony is the Indian mango tree that Hind may once have climbed. Perhaps Sahla followed her, though she was more nervous than her sister. Through the iron railing the two of them would have spied the strokes of his paintbrush as it filled in drawings he had copied from the murals in the tombs where a German archaeological team was working. They could hear fillies whinnying in the stable and dogs howling in the distance, but they were not afraid.

After a while Pierre packed his bags, tore up quite a few of his paintings, and told the Basha that he was leaving for Al-Kafra or Fazan to discover the old caravan roads. He said that he had despaired of ever imitating the engravings in the houses of the dead. The Basha shook his head and spoke of Jidd Minazi' who used to travel there with caravans bearing wheat, salt and cloth. When he departed Pierre left behind many unfinished paintings.

They brought back the box without its owner, and Hind dragged it into her room and kept the little scraps of paper. Years later Muhra poured over it and tried to decipher its symbols. They were not diaries as she had thought at first, just as Pierre with the blue eyes was not what she had imagined him to be. The picture of his face, which was repeated in his many attempts to draw himself, showed a pale, sallow young man. Abu Shreek told her that he was as yellow as turmeric; his hair was cut short around his bald patch and his body skinny and weak. Judging from a photograph of him sitting next to Abu Shreek resting his face on the palm of his hand as he stared into the flames of their camp fire, his fingers were his most distinguished feature.

Nobody knew why he came. Some said he was accompanying the German team that had arrived to search for ancient buried treasure but he did not work with them. Those who had delved more deeply into the matter said that he bought a bundle of Pharaonic manuscripts from the Basha that old Jidd Minazi', who had been with Dorvetti at Tel Al-Maskhouta, used to hang from his tent pole. Dorvetti, who was looking for mummies, said they used the papyri to cure their sick, and he was always finding such scrolls between the legs of the dead. Jidd Minazi' kept one and hung it in a pouch on the wall of his tent because burning them brought bad luck, while preserving them frightened away evil spirits.

He related the tale of the well at Hedaywa where they used to draw water during their trips. At the bottom of the well were stones with Pharaonic symbols on them. The water of the well was so clear that whoever hung his head over the edge could see the carvings as if they were right under his nose. After that it became their custom to throw those stones, which the ancient Egyptians had charged with magical power, into their wells, because they had the effect of alum or mastic, and made the water as clear as silver. The Jidd who hung up the scroll believed that they struck fear into the hearts of genies, and deflected the evil eye. Monsieur Arkan, who was head of the German expedition to the Laqaya Hills, said that they were spells used by the dead to bring solace during their long isolation and to petition the God. The Jidd nodded his head and said that they keep away the worms too. "Have you not seen their corpses?" he asked, "They remain forever like a smooth piece of wood."

When Pierre turned up some time later and said that he was a relative of Monsieur Arkan, the Basha offered him a place to stay in the pavilion. He told Pierre that the Monsieur was their dear friend, had hunted with the Jidd in the desert and shot wild rabbits with a catapult. Then he pointed to a picture hanging in the centre of the reception room, which showed the gentleman seated next to the Jidd at the head of the *majlis* sipping coffee. The Basha was delighted with the pipe Pierre gave him because it was made of pure ivory, and the black ebony stick was also exquisite. But they did not know for how many boxes of cartridges Pierre Kamm took that papyrus painted by the Ancient Egyptians. The Basha kept his stick proudly by his side as he talked about Wad Madani and Naqawa and his grandfathers' journeys to the land of gold. Muhra never found the papyrus, but she did discover, in a pouch of gazelle skin hanging in an old tamarisk tree, a drawing which appeared to be a copy of it.

Pierre would frequent the expedition's excavations for days at a time, copying the murals and sending detailed reports to the Egyptian Archaeological Society about the nature of the investigation and the degree of permanence of the colours. He ceased doing this after a while though, and instead became absorbed in drawing many of the faces that were around him. Pierre appeared to be no more than an amateur who had accompanied different expeditions and all that Muhra found were superficial observations and some plans of the excavation. As she unfolded more of the papers on which he had recorded disconnected sentences and drawn sketches, she was able to guess that the man with the smooth-shaven European face sitting in a boat on a raging ocean and the woman with drawn features wearing red slippers and a ruffled dress in the style of the early century, were in fact his mother and father.

On the back he had written: "Because he loved the smell of seaweed he was always travelling. She sat in front of the fire knitting a shawl for the winter without a man, while he brought coffee from Yemen, tea from India, gold from Naqawa and slaves from Kago. When I became a young man carrying reams of paper under my arm in an attempt to draw her face, he used to tell me about the honour of working in the navy. I continued to paint pictures of women that looked like her."

There is a drawing of Miss Martine's face with its pronounced features. She is seated on a camel and dressed in a woollen *abaya* and *igal*. She may be on one of her trips to the temple at Abu Simbel. The picture suggests a feisty young woman and her expression is a blend of female and male. The young features turn into an old woman sitting behind a table holding in her hand a copy of her book, *My Journey to the Orient*, She is resting her head on the hard granite face of Hatshepsut which she has placed in front of her. Miss Martine used to say that Hatshepsut was the first traveller in history and in her temple is a mural depicting her glorious journey to the Land of Punt. Fuelled with a desire for adventure, Miss Martine took up her pens, and set off with a number of amateur artists who saw in the Ancient Egyptian monuments precise measurements and a deep awareness of perspective and balance. They drew the basic lines of the Hall of Columns and the Avenue of Rams as they travelled by steamer towards Abu Simbel and the Island of Philae. They spent the night dancing to the humming of river mosquitoes and wandered around in the day sketching the monuments as they discussed Champolion and Sir Gardener Wilkinson, and Carter. Their dream was that one of their camels would stumble on the rocky ground of the West Bank at Luxor. Underground chambers belonging to ancient temples would open up and they would inscribe their names on them. They would return bearing the sarcophagus of the Queen of Punt, or discover the secret of eternal life in the amulet of Mart-Ser-Qut, Lover of Silence, Goddess of the cemeteries at Thebes, whose jet black frog-like form brought great good fortune. But all that Miss Martine brought back was conversation about the desert rocks that looked like red gold and the gradually changing shades of the sand dunes, and the yellowness of the apricot flowers against the endless expanse of sky blue and Nile mercury. She called it the colour symbolism of Ancient Egypt and spoke of the secret of the russet and yellow pigments with which they dyed the bodies of the dead so that they would take on the hue of the desert which the Nile restored to life every fertility cycle. And she described in considerable detail how much she enjoyed the journey because her donkey had a fine English saddle and they had sailed on a Thomas Cook steamer.

Her house was packed with sarcophagi and antiques, small statues and trinkets that she had bought from the Arabs for a string of beads or a piece of silver. She had donated the money to the Egyptian Archaeological Society which sent Pierre to prepare a full account of the tombs. He started to write his descriptions but never sent them to her. Instead he wrote her letters expounding the theory of colour symbolism he had begun to develop. For him the recently opened tombs represented nothing more than corpses, dead people who wanted to traverse the heavens and be transformed into eternal stars never setting. The bodies whose organs had been stored in canopic jars: heart, intestines, liver, stomachs stuffed with perfume, and the linen bandages wrapped round the corpses made him tear up what he had drawn, and write to Miss Martine about other things more worthy of investigation, such as life and death for example.

"I've painted vultures," he wrote to her, "swooping down, beaks at the ready, on the corpse of a camel that had expired on some desert track. They descend all at once, densely packed, sweeping away everything in their path, like greedy and expectant beneficiaries at the reading of a will, flapping their wings in skirmish, haggling over the rotting cadaver. They leave mere bones in their wake, and when the rains fall the skeleton will turn white and brittle, like the ones encountered by travellers to reassure them that they are following the right track through the desert and that caravans have indeed passed this way before them."

And about the merchants he wrote: "They move with their caravans at night, so it is said, carrying water with them and find their way by the stars as sailors do. The guide observes the movement of the heavens and talks about distant stars as if they were maps by which he plots his course."

Pierre drew lots of faces which they found at the bottom of his box. There was Al-Najdiyya on her rug on the balcony taking her snuff; the wash tub with the little bodies gathered round scrubbing clothes, their skirts rolled up over their legs, sweat dripping between their breasts; men in *kufiyyas* trudging over dusty tracks amid wide mud houses and yards with high walls that kept out the sky. As they scrutinised the pictures carefully, trying to work out who the drawings were of, they would guess that this was Abu Shreek Al-Iyadi's nose or that the dark skin of Mubarak the slave.

He had painted a number of pictures of falcons speeding after nervous rabbits, and gazelles hiding having left faint hoof marks on the sand to reveal where they had gone. There was Hind with the cat's face in the pose she had assumed after slipping up the branches of the mango tree, climbing onto the balcony, slinking quietly over to where he lay and licking his feet and fingers which were the colour of turmeric. He smiled as he dozed and held her close. She buried her head in his chest, and their breaths mingled as they slumbered happily together.

Then Muhra came across pictures of another woman in the bottom of Pierre's box, who was not Hind or Miss Martine or his mother. This woman had the neck of the fabled Al-Jaziya and a hair style like Layla Murad. Surely Hind who had sorted through the box more than once must have seen the drawings of this face. She had tied up those papers in a lock of hair. They said she used to cry a lot and sit on a branch of the mango tree clutching a bundle of papers to her breast. They all thought they were the pages of the novel her brother had torn up. Even so, Hind never removed the leather cord with the eye of magic ivory hanging from it. Muhra found it in an old leather document case hidden by the woman with the neck of noble Al-Jaziya. Now she sits alone on the balcony watching the mewing cats, waiting to see if Hind will pass like she used to, and lick her feet and purr. She hugs the folder which contains the photo of the three young girls who used to sit beneath the veranda by the earthenware water jugs. There were other things in the portfolio too, though they were less important: a picture of the uncle on the mother's side, a love amulet, some recipes for *makbousa*, instructions for storing mango juice, and ways of making marmalade and home-made ice cream. Next to the documents and pictures in the bottom of the cupboard were half-empty bottles of perfume, and although they appeared never to have been used at all, the contents had evaporated. Small notes, dated long ago, were attached to them addressed to "my darling wife" and "my dear cousin," or simply "sweetheart." On the shelf above were dresses with low neck lines, underskirts of starched tulle, and sets of pink satin lingerie sewn by Miss Angela. Sahla had never worn any of them.

10

—-—

When Abu Shreek Al-Iyadi came past, and sat down by
the ashes where her father used to stand his coffee pot,
Muhra rested her head on the balcony rail.

"Do you know the *gunfus* bird?" he asked.

"No," she said.

"It used to fly around us," he replied, "as we crossed the
rocky terrain by the river bed strewn with pebbles. People
used to say it had the sweetest voice of any bird. Pierre would
take out the papers he kept in a gazelle-skin pouch and sit
some distance away so he could write. We crossed the red
steppes and a scorching expanse of soft sand, then followed
the route used by the caravans to bring ostrich feathers, ivory
and slaves. We headed westward from Aswan through the
Oasis of Karar, Dongola and the Hidden Wells, but we did
not reach the well of Sulayma by the old road. Pierre wanted
to visit Barbar, Shindi and Sinnar too, and even the slave
markets on the Gold Coast."

Abu Shreek said all this then stood up to leave, picking up his stick that had an old horsehair snare tied to one end.

"It sings for seven days in a voice that will steal your heart," he said, rubbing the mist of distant days from his eyes before adding, "Then it falls down dead."

"What does?" asked Muhra.

"The *gunfus* bird," he replied.

He walked to the tamarisk tree on the hill where he lived, or Al-Alawaya as everyone called it. It was the place where Inshirah used to hide when the soldiers came. Behind it runs the Minazi' canal full of expired corpses dumped there long ago and fragments of memories. He drew together the threads that were scattered around him and spat on the palms of his hands. Then he twisted them tightly together, making sure to keep them slender and strong and tied them into seamless circles like disks of wax. Once the bird's feet went through them they would not come out again; the more the bird pulled, the more the threads would tighten. He was skilled at making traps and selecting the choicest strands of hair from fillies' tails, which he kept in his pouch in case he needed to repair the snare. There were always some young men at his house watching him work as he told them about Sharrafa, daughter of the Al-Bashariyya tribe, whom Jidd Minazi' had brought back with him, or Khashm Al-Mous, one of the Kings of Sudan, and the six slaves of clan Al-Shafei. The lads would gape in wonder as he twisted the threads and stretched them out.

"Whose son are you, boy?" he would often ask.

The young men had grown tired of recounting their genealogies, which he always forgot anyway, and even if he did remember, he might mention something they did not like to hear. He still retained his sharp eyesight and a memory for things long ago that could not be faulted, though every patch of his skin was buried beneath the wrinkles that had closed in on his eyes and crowded round his straight nose and his tight mouth.

Abu Shreek takes some paper packets out of the pocket of his old overcoat, then unfolds them. He places his little pot on the fire and waits for the coffee to boil. A blend of spicy smells floats on the air around his plastic containers, some of which are empty and some full of water. He chews a few datura leaves, rolls a cigarette, then folds up the paper packets and puts them back in his pocket. The boys scurry over the hill, looking among the hedgehogs, and the cactus plants, and the mountain mosses for other kinds of leaves that grow here and there. They smoke with him slowly, and when they feel like annoying him, they say: "You're just a camel herder." He stresses that he was a caravan guide, not a camel herder, but they don't see a great difference. He resumes the story he began earlier, about how he used to lead the Hajj caravan from Egypt to Al-Qaseer, and how he accompanied Dorvetti with Old Minazi' to the Ancient Egyptian tombs near Tel Al-Maskhouta when the way there was untamed wilderness and no one ever thought to take it; and that he had been many times to the Place Where the Rivers Meet, and the Golden Tributary.

They don't completely believe him but they listened on. They gather round so he can teach them how to set a snare, and tie the twisted threads into loops so they will tighten round the bird's leg and it can't get away. As they run back down the hill and leave him to his solitude, flirting with phantoms, he asks them again: "Whose son are you, boy?" so he can try to link the father with the grandfather and construct a family tree that no one can remember anymore. He sometimes spends his day walking between the walls of the village, carrying his long spear with an even longer string tied to it and his snare fluttering at the end like the kites the little boys make. He says he's hunting but nothing falls in the snare except a few stalks of straw from the fields. Sometimes the snare gets snagged in the branch of a sesban tree at the edge of a field and he tugs the thread angrily and snaps it. Then he picks up the broken threads and weaves them back together.

The threads of the stories he tells are more complex than the ones he weaves with his hands, that is, if there is anyone to listen to him. He likes nothing more than to wipe the saliva from the corner of his mouth with his sleeve. Half his teeth are missing but his mouth is full of details, and when he speaks he repeats things so that Muhra the daughter of Al-Shafei can understand. He leans his head against the wrought iron balcony railing finished with wood and shares cups of coffee with Amma Mizna, who doesn't pay any attention to what he says unless he makes a grave mistake which needs correcting: that it's not possible to count the wives and sons of Al-Shafei, for example, that the girl Jidd Mahjoub threw into the river so she wouldn't marry a peasant, even if he was the red-faced Turk, was really called Asrana, and not Khayaliyya as he claimed, or that Minazi' did not marry a girl from the Al-Bashariyya tribe but one from the Al-Shayegiyya, who were the guardians of the land of Al-Bijja and relatives of Bani Sulaym. Muhra does not care too much for such details but she watches his mouth, which trembles as he pours out the stories. Her eyes follow him as he hobbles towards the door leaning on his stick and disappears behind the wall that surrounds the mango and orange gardens and the deserted stables. On the gulf of soft sand where the young men gather at sunset to relax, resting their heads on their elbows as the scent of their smoking blends with the aroma of boiling coffee, they watch Abu Shreek as he walks towards them. The string of thread tied to his stick blows left and right in the wind like a fishhook of palm frond that the boys would be ashamed to fish with in the canal. He approaches slowly and scrutinises their faces.

"Arabs or peasants?" he asks, in all seriousness.

The young men, who have grown sick and tired of repeating their genealogies, may laugh as they stand the coffee pots among the embers and melt pieces of opium in the boiling liquid. While one blows on the fire, another says: "May Allah be pleased with you, *Ya* Jidd, go and find someone else to sit with." The boy who hands him the cup of coffee is dark skinned, dressed in a white *thobe* and has thrown his *kufiyya* up over his head. Abu Shreek inspects his face. He does not ask him whose son he is but regales him with a much more direct question:

"Are you descended from the slaves of Al-Minazi' or Al-Shafei, boy?" The handsome youth says nothing, just exhales his smoke. Discomfort reigns, then silence.

Abu Shreek refuses to give up. "Are you the son of Mubarak the slave?"

The boy grows more uneasy, and his irritation only increases with everyone else's silence. "Mubarak is my grandfather," he replies.

Abu Shreek swallows proudly as he tries to remember exactly: "Then your great grandfather is Khashm Al-Mous. Minazi' brought him up from the Sudan, near the Place Where the Waters Meet. There were ten slaves and he settled them west of the Bedouin lands. Khashm Al-Mous was like you, *Ya* Bin Mubarak. He had the eyes of a young fox."

Everyone laughs, except the boy.

"Minazi' always used to tell him: 'Slave, you have the smell of a fox.'"

They laugh again then there is silence.

"And what is your father doing, *Ya* Bin Mubarak?" Abu Shreek continues.

"He's at home. He has some guests. He's selling them falcons."

"Do they wear *igals*, boy, or are they city folk?"

"They're Kuwaitis, *Ya* Jidd."

"How many birds have you caught this year, boy?"

"Three, *Ya* Jidd."

Abu Shreek Al-Iyadi nods his head and pours the dregs of his cup onto the embers. He would like to talk more about Khashm Al-Mous, and Rawda, and Inshirah and the slave caravans that came up from Harar, but he senses he should go. He stumbles along, holding himself up against the mud walls, and gets lost among the narrow alleys. He does not know how to find his way to the sandy land beyond the houses, to the hill and his old tamarisk tree. The concrete buildings that are lined up in tall rows reveal nothing. Behind them is the highway where the cars speed past. They never stop to ask an old caravan guide about Roaring Lion Well or the wild lands of Al-Bajja.

He wanders aimlessly for a while and pauses to catch his breath against many walls as he tries to retrace landmarks that no longer exist. Only the dizziness accompanies him. For several nights now he has been feeling it, something he can sense but not understand. It has begun not only to accompany him but to assault his memory. It leads him to believe that he has seen all this before. He had heard a lot about the luminous figures, men who sip coffee with dignity and ask you how you are then disappear like a mirage that melts into the blazing trackless desert. He had prepared himself to exchange stories with his ghosts and not annoy them, but women are washing clothes nearby and a smell of detergent fills his head, mixed with the odour of fungus and lime. It is the stench of a damp grave that has just been opened to receive a new arrival. The feeling that he has lived all these events before takes a stronger hold, and all he can do is let his legs move round and round in circles. He stops in the middle of the street totally lost. He stands for a long time leaning against the wall while he works out that, if he goes down this road, it will lead him to the high cliff where Amma Mizna lives. Or will he stumble out of it into the Laqaya Hills where the German expedition have their camp. Will he find the home of Al-Minazi' at the end of the road or the houses of the sons of Al-Shafei? He looks around and turns to ask the passers by: "Whose house is this, sweetheart?" and "Whose place is that, *Ya* Shiekh Al-Arab?" And even though they answer him in detail about their genealogies and the owners of the homes behind the closed doors, he cannot place them on the old maps in his head, of the former Bedouin estate, that he had known when it was no more than a swathe of sand, and he knew everybody's forebears right back to the very first Jidd.

Abu Shreek brings together the threads that have almost come to an end.

They had set off from Assiut heading west, he tells Muhra. They passed Roaring Lion Well on the first day but the water there was salty and they could not take provision of it. Their caravan was made up of five camels which they had loaded with supplies. Pierre's she-camel was more weighed down than the others, as it was carrying his many chests. For three whole days they travelled through arid desert, which Abu Shreek had crossed a thousand times before. He knew its rabbit holes and lizards' lairs, had counted every *ghardag* tree on its hills, and run behind the gazelles until the soles of his feet had cracked from its scorching surface. Lost in their camel songs they did not notice the trail gradually fading. The next day revealed only bright blood-red sand. They had assumed that on the third day, after crossing Wadi Zaydoun with its huge lifeless boulders, the horizon would open up onto the low land, and the Hidden Wells with their sweet refreshing water would come into view and they would be able to replenish their skins. They scanned the land around them for any sign they might recognise. The hills of sand that Wadi Zaydoun led into seemed to stretch forever and their feet sank into the red dunes as if they trudged through seas of soft flour. The more they ploughed on, the more parched the land became, and the five beasts grew weary of searching for any scrap of vegetation to chew.

Pierre, who was content to withdraw with his papers to draw or write whenever they made camp, was opposed to the idea of turning back. The sea of sand under which the Hidden Wells had been submerged gave way on the fourth day to stone and gravel. They began to notice traces of pus and blood on the pebbles that was dripping from the first she-camel and they had to leave it behind. When they returned, the carcass was one of the signs that guided them on their way. They transferred the chests to another hump, lightened them by throwing away the clothes in his rucksack, abandoned a number of his paintings and got rid of the medicine for headaches, diarrhoea and vomiting. Now thirst had become the most immediate threat to their survival. What eventually forced them to turn back however was not the camels but the route. For although they had observed Sirius crossing the sky, and the constellation of Al-Nathra setting in the west, and their compass had allowed them to determine their direction, the Hidden Wells did not materialise, nor did the Valley of Stones reveal the well of Al-Sultan as they had expected. From this point on all they saw were the vast red flat lands whose cruel sands flew up and tore relentlessly at their eyes. Pierre was forced to throw his glasses away after the sands had scratched them beyond repair and he could no longer see through them. All he could do was bury his face in his headscarf and pull his *igal* down over his head. He threw away his shoes and put on leather sandals. When Al-Nathra swung towards the north with Orion in the south and Gazelle Tracks clearly visible in the vast night sky, they counted again the number of nights they had been travelling. They beseeched Allah to protect them from the dark omen of that constellation, knowing full well that it was a presage of separation. But the clouds of dust distracted them while the sweat that poured from Pierre's brow turned to burning fever that dampened cloths could not assuage. They fixed up a wooden frame on one of the camel's backs and tied the ropes fast around him. They realised now that they would have to head back as quickly as possible, not just to save him, but for fear that the same fate would overtake them, as their water skins emptied one after the other.

The camels swayed from side to side and the men's soft songs mingled with his delirium as it grew more audible. When Gazelle Tracks ascended directly above them, a star shimmering in the sky with her frightened young ones running nervously behind her, they took him down and laid him on the sand. It was there where the water hole they called the Hidden Wells had been, the very spot they had passed a few days before.

All they found in his pouch was a papyrus that Pierre had bought from Lamloum Basha. They left it there, hanging from a tent pole to frighten the wraiths that wander the wilderness. If they had opened it they would have found houses and alley ways and birds and ducks swimming on the river, a herdsman crossing the plain with his flock, a woman breastfeeding her child on the far bank, a crocodile stretching his head towards the fisherman's boat, a frog made of soft clay resting its head in long slumber. Whenever Muhra sits down to decipher the symbols on the copy she has, she notices that the herdsman who sits on the bank of the river looks like one of

93

her grandfathers who used to walk through hills that were the colour of yellow-ochre or tinged with the redness of dusk, and she sees camels crossing the desert like distant ships twinkling in the emptiness. She might even see the tracks of a timorous antelope or the skeleton of a long-dead she-camel, or perhaps embers where coffee once brewed smelling of the far away land of Punt.